Places to Be

A Young Adult Novel

For 5th grade and up and as well as adults

Alvin L.A. Horn

PLACES TO BE
A Young Adult Novel

Alvin L.A. Horn
Romantic Blues Publishing
Seattle, Washington
Copyright © 2022 Alvin L.A. Horn
All Rights Reserved

Cover concept and layout: Alvin L.A. Horn
Front and back cover artwork: Lena Janelle, Art By Lena J

www.alvinhorn.com
Romantic Blues Publishing
Seattle, Washington
Paperback ISBN:
Hardback ISBN:

Dear Reader,

The "Sankofa Bird" is a mythical bird that flies with its head backward. It is from the Akan people in West Africa. One definition/meaning: "to go back and fetch." It also depicts the bird having an egg in its mouth that symbolizes the present and future generations of young people to come.

Mr. Alvin Horn's book provides an excellent opportunity for young adults to learn, understand, and embrace the rich trials and challenges they will face. During their transition from young adults to adulthood, they will indeed have many opportunities to practice what they have learned as they navigate their rich transformation process.

Being an educator, too often, I have witnessed and experienced young adults struggling with the subject of "history" in both middle and high school settings. I feel it's primarily because they don't "see themselves" in the "stories." Also, how are our children's lives enhanced when there is a healthy intervention? (A mysterious elder librarian places the "right" volumes of history into Marley's hands).

Once our children are exposed to specific historical information, it creates awareness, curiosity, critical inquiry, which (I feel) leads to self-discovery. These self-discoveries are rooted in creating a positive self-image and the ability to imagine and visualize their self-efficacy.

Mr. Horn strategically uses the importance of using rich ancestral histories to captivate the reader and provide life lessons centered around perseverance, courage, resilience, and personal triumphs.

This fictional book is a must-read for young adults who share an interest in getting to know people from different periods of time through a willingness to time travel the earth through some characters that surely can be a manifestation of themselves!

—*Mr. Delbert Richardson,* Ethnomuseumologist, second-generation storyteller of the *national award-winning,* The Unspoken Truths American History Traveling Museum

Marley leads the next generation on a magnificent journey of discovery across time and place! Mr. Horn, a writer who transcends genres, has entered the young adult fiction world with memorable characters, experiences, and wonder. Places to Be is the book we have been waiting for. It speaks to intergenerational connections between youth and elders, profound parental love, and shared humanity. Young urban Black youth will recognize their lived experiences in the characters and settings in this wandering voyage marked by many changes of fortune. I recommend this book to schools, educators, youth organizations, public libraries. Please put a copy in the hands of every young person in your life.

Anita Koyier-Mwamba, JD. Manager of *Black Education*, Seattle Public Schools. Mom of a young adult daughter and a young teen son.

Mr. Horn has been a valuable member of our school community for years. He has worked with students' families and community to grow our children, teaching them life lessons along the way. His literary stories ring true through his journeys as a teacher, coach, and parent. Whether discussing the history of Seattle or connecting about current events in the world, Alvin LA Horn is a storyteller that deserves to be noticed. Sit back and enjoy!

Justin Hendrickson,
Principal *at South Shore PK-8*
Seattle, Washington

Reading Alvin "LA" Horn evokes the same feelings as listening to Miles Davis' horn. It's soulful, truthful, rapturous, and spectacularly unique. Our younger generations are fortunate to have Horn use his energetic verve to bring them a story of timeless wisdom in an accessible and entertaining manner. In fact, anyone who picks up his book can share in that fortune!

- Marcus Harrison Green, author of *Readying to Rise*
Seattle, journalist and essayist - editor-in-chief and of the
South Seattle Emerald

"Alvin L. Horn is a genius writer. His writings are poetic. His storytelling is an intro for a thriller that leaves you wondering if you were there in the flesh—one of the characters. The suspense Alvin L.A. Horn writes is moving, powerful, and causes you to search inner vulnerabilities when you read into characters' lives as they live on the edge. Alvin's writing is just as poignant... Tender, emotional, thoughtful, and socially conscious. I'm a true fan. I'd read anything he wrote."

-Suzetta Perkins, bestselling author,

Two Down: The Inconvenient Truth, Hollywood Skye

"Alvin L.A. Horn's written words and spoken word have proven to be, for me, transforming, infusing, invigorating, replenishing, and inspiring to my soul. He gives life and uplifts life through his words. Alvin's writings transport the reader to places known and unknown. However, additionally, this cerebral experience and the journey one takes with him, is felt on a positive instinctual level, as well. One very personal experience I have had in reading Alvin's books and becoming voluntarily enmeshed in Alvin's prolific and incomparable writings is they caused me to react physically and emotionally while experiencing challenging situations. This novel is a must-read!

"Alvin L.A. Horn keeps you on the edge of what is going to happen. Everything is tense situations laced in, realistic mayhem, and secrets, mixed with social commentary through dealings and dialogue. I love moral justice. I highly recommend this book to those who love literature. You will learn and expand your reasoning."

- Corey Minor Smith, the author of *Driven and Canton City Councillor at Large*, Canton, OH

"Whenever Alvin L.A. Horn creates something from the hillsides out there on the West Coast, in Seattle, Washington, I always know he will give us another taste of his uniquely diverse experiences. From today's young adults to all readers of any age, he never fails. Alvin L.A Horn gives it to us again in real, possible images that are thoughtful, full of knowledge and wisdom."

- *Omar Tyree*, New York Times bestselling author, NAACP Image Award winner

Alvin L.A. Horn has intertwined a sensitive and captivating story in Places to Be with imaginative real-like characters who might be in any one person we might know. Through intense, straightforward storytelling, the writer pushes us onto the fictional and mythical but scholarly stage between the covers of this young adult book that all ages will enjoy. With attention to detail, the author colors the room with facts conversations while on a journey through time. The reader will hear the sounds and see to become one with the uncertainties of what is real and what is not and prevails over fears at the same time as the characters Marley and Alana. The story feels real for all of us when we were once all teenagers in this suspenseful novel. I am genuinely a fan of this author's writing style.

- *Roxann McCoy*
President, NAACP Las Vegas
"Our Lives Begin to End The Day We Become Silent About Things That Matter" Dr. Martin Luther King

Alvin L.A. Horn is a rare literary gem whose talent surpasses what is commonplace in many literary offerings. His ability to create art; paint a vivid narrative with his skill in incredible storytelling ranks him amongst my favorite authors. Heart-wrenching, poignant, engrossing, and hard to put down, Places to Be will take you on a literary ride of entertaining cultured knowledge."

- Elissa Gabrielle,
Award-winning Author of A Whisper to a Scream

Alvin L. A. Horn's young adult novel speaks to the heart of coming-of-age urban youth experiences. Alvin is best known for his award-winning work in other genres. However, this swivel to young adult fiction is rife with excitement. It is filled with adventure, wit, moral contemplation as it transports a young teen to a world of wonder. Marley time travels and finds himself at the cross-roads of humanity's most challenging moral and ethical crossroads. The story is set in urban Seattle and captures the dawning of young adulthood in a setting rarely captured in books-the story of young Black teens who are loved, have multiple options in life and successfully negotiate cross cultural and intergenerational relationships.

Marley is a star hooper, a good student and comes from a family that loves him. Like many middle schoolers, that combination of character makes him popular and highly regarded. While with friends, Marley finds himself in the company of friends who make a poor choice. That choice impacts him and leads him to a summer of maturity.

This book identifies themes of peer pressure, exploration of friendship, examination of identity, identification of talent and the power of imagination. The book explores history and compels the reader to consider the basis of moral and ethical decision-making. As a life-long educator, I encourage every student and adult to read this book. Through this book youth will see their connection to the past and be inspired to imagine themselves in the future.

Romantic Blues Publishing
Seattle Washington

Dear Reader, a word from the author Alvin L.A. Horn:

What a pleasure it is to share with you the timeless characters in this young adult novel. *Places to Be* is set during present day and time-travels to other historic periods and places through possible scenarios, not factual engagements that any of us could know. This novel is a moving, tangled web of history that will have meaning for anyone. Told through two teenagers, Marly Barton Tingle and Alana Kona-Parks, this a chronicle of startling events through books they read.

Places to Be shines brightness on narratives of the past, so readers become aware of aspects of history that teach values from other times and places. These can be used in present times to think about and then to do the right thing, when it comes to leadership, family, and friendships.

These days, most of us have relatives like a parent, grandparent, or even great-grands of family members, who have shared oral histories. In this book, oral histories become visual, full of places and characters in the context of how they lived their lives, including the surrounding culture and atmospheres. As Marly and Alana, peer deep into history, they are witnesses to a dynamic assembly of characters and situations.

As always, thank you for supporting the efforts ofof my writings. I strive to bring you fresh and groundbreaking stories that will help you escape reality when life seems overwhelming or whenever you just want to visit another time and place. I appreciate the love and dedication of my new and past readers.

Alvin L.A. Horn

Chapter 1

*O*uch! *Oh, that hurts.* I have fallen out of bed.

I was tossing and turning. Now, I feel pain in my tailbone. Must've been another bad dream where I heard my mom's voice in my head from a couple of days ago and saw her angry face. I feel my stomach turning, same as when Mom confronted me.

It is way past midnight, and I can't fall back to sleep. I still feel pinned across from her, and I'm sweating again just thinking about it...

Mom stared at me. I was frozen in place. I wanted to be anyplace but in her fierce storm of words. She had that rare look that always meant I was in trouble.

"Don't say a word." Her voice chilled me to the bone.

I stood across from her at the dining room table, shifting my weight back and forth in my feet, but not so's she could see.

"*Marley Barton Tingle!* I'm not raising you to act a fool at school. And how could you exploit yourself as if you don't have the good sense? We have raised you to have *pride* in all you do, but naaaah you out here in public, soiling your good name?" She took a breath, but I knew I wasn't supposed to answer any of that. Then she added, "What kinds of friends do you have that did what they did? And don't you *dare* act as if you didn't know what they were up to...!"

I'm officially grounded from all the fun things I had planned.

I throw my covers on the floor, trying to cool down from my fire hot nightmare. And this is just the beginning. I'm about to live a nightmare for my whole entire summer.

"Marley Barton Tingle, what is all that noise?" she shouts from down the hall. "You should be in bed and asleep by now. If you are up, go to bed!"

Of course, she heard when I fell out of bed. It's not something I have ever done before. And I knocked a glass of water off my nightstand and onto the hardwood floor. It made even more noise when it shattered. Now I have to clean it up before I cut myself.

I can't recall the last time I had such a bad dream. Clearly, I am freaked out with my mom being so mad at me for what I did... and what I *didn't* do.

I'm not a bad kid. I come home late sometimes and might have conveniently forgotten to give her the full details about something that happened, when she asked. So, I had been optimistic, even when my mom was going off on me, that she would only put me on punishment for a few days. Maybe just let me off with a warning.

Boy, was I wrong.

My mom is a tall, beautiful woman who was born in Jamaica. She migrated to America when she received a college scholarship to run track. My friends always say, respectfully, that my mom is pretty, and they love talking to her because of her lilting accent and because she is smart and super-friendly.

Mom earned her degree in optometry, although people tried to hold her down because she had dark skin and an unusual accent. After all she has experienced, I believe her when she says she had to work harder to overcome those who made roadblocks for her.

She believes in chances. She expects the best from me...

But I have failed in her eyes.

Chapter 2

I was hanging out with my friends before going home after the last day of school. I was with Carlos, Devon, Sheva, and A-Mm, as she calls herself, and we stopped off at the Dime to Dollar Store for some snacks.

While we were there, they shoplifted. I didn't know beforehand what they were going to do. Yes, I did go to the store without permission, but I did not think it was a big deal, even though my parents constantly repeat this mantra, "Little things can turn into big things."

So now I wonder, really, why are my parents coming down so hard on me? I didn't take anything…

Maybe I did think my friends were acting funny before we went inside the store. And it's true, they avoided me once we went through the door and started down the aisles. But it was only later that I learned they had been stealing. *I definitely* didn't take anything, though. I paid for my candy.

The store cameras caught them, and it was not the first time, as their parents let it be known. I thought I knew my friends better, but as Mom said, "To understand the meaning, you cannot read a book by its cover."

I was guilty by association, just for being in the store with them.

If only I had ridden the school bus straight home after school, maybe I wouldn't be in so much trouble.

One week after school let out for the summer, my mom opened the front door to find the police on our doorstep. They handed her a letter that said I was not allowed to enter the store again or I would be charged with trespassing.

I will never forget the look on my mother's face as she confronted me that evening. Her eyes penetrated me, making me feel immediately nervous. I had hurt my mom in the worst way. After the police came to our house concerning my wrongdoing, her eyes dripped tears onto the letter as she stared down at the words. Then she went to the window and beckoned me to join her.

The two officers were standing outside, chuckling.

She took a deep breath and said, "Marley, my worst nightmare is the police coming to our door. Whether it be about your father or you and or your sisters, it is never good. *Never*!" She rubbed her temples as she passed me the note to read for myself.

The letter said the store owners had captured me coming into the store on camera. It showed me with my friends, who stole goods while they were there. My friends' parents received the same police knock on their door, so, right away, the parents all called one another.

While my mom was on the phone, she stared into my eyes, and I felt her tear-filled eyes burn flames through me.

I hurt my mother. I didn't steal, but I did share and trade candy with my friends. I think I knew they had shoplifted by the time we got to the park, but I didn't care, because I'd done nothing wrong. Still, I messed up, thinking it was no big deal, so I'm in trouble.

My grades are pretty good. I don't get in any school kind of trouble often. I do daydream in class, and I have had a few after-school detentions because of not paying attention or turning my work in late sometimes. But then my final middle-school grades went online for my mom to see on the same day those policemen came to our door.

I did not finish a report in my history class... Well, I never started writing the essay... End-of-school-year activities like dances, field trips, and select all-star basketball became my priority. That and being lazy led to a regretful history grade.

I don't understand how these olden times from back in the day, long before I was born, really have anything to do with school and what we need to study. And history class seems to make us do more reading and writing on top of all the other reading and writing we do for the other classes.

I can see how math matters. I need to be able to count my money, if I ever have a chance to turn pro. My language arts grade was not much better, and that was from being lazy, too. But I understand how language arts class can help me talk and write in a way people will listen to me. Plus, I love to write. But I almost failed that class, too.

Still, *why history?* Why should I care about what date something happened? Or who invented the traffic light, just so long as it works? Then, we have to study all the horrible stuff countries and people did—but does it matter now? So what that slave ships brought my great-great-great-great grandparent to the Islands and America 400 years ago? I don't even know the names of my people from *five* generations ago. And the other stuff they teach...? Like, why do we have to study maps when we have GPS?

Chapter 3

Mom called my dad, who is in Germany on a job, and told him all about what had happened.

"Son," he said when I got on the line, "I back everything mom has laid out for how it will be this summer. You know me. I typically let your mom say how it will be. I often go to bat for you, too, but not this time. I'm upset with you."

I heard the anger in my dad's voice. He always told me anger is the hurt you feel. My behavior hurt my dad's feelings. Generally, he is cool with an old-school swag that says, "Let's keep the peace."

I betrayed the love he and my mom sent my way to protect me. I ignored the most important thing my parents taught me: respecting myself and respecting my family.

"Son, you need to be on restriction for the whole summer, despite the fact it might hurt your basketball game the first year. You are just about to go into high school. Important time!"

"But Dad, Coach Barker at the high school came to see me play in middle school, and I had my best game. The coach said he was looking forward to me playing for him. But he mentioned I had to get stronger, so I *need* to work out."

"No, you need to be a man who acts right and avoids the obvious wrongs." Dad's deep, measured voice felt like he was reaching inside me and squeezing. "Oh, when I get back, I will run you harder than you can imagine, if you think I'll let you turn out for basketball."

As I stood there, all I could imagine was what my dad would have me do in his fierce workouts, once he came home.

"You will pass *my* fitness test," he continued. "Your mom's punishment, well, that's one thing. My punishment will build some character, as soon as I get back. We raised you to make much better choices, and there is always a cost for bad judgments." My dad's voice is usually like a tuba playing all low notes, but today, it sounded strangely high from his own anger at me.

He still had more to say to me. "One of the reasons I need you to get this lesson and get it right is reflected in what Martin Luther King, Jr. said, *'Those who sit idly by, they are a part of the problem.'* He wrote a letter to the pastors of White churches while he was in jail for protesting for the lack of civil rights. It was called 'Letter from a Birmingham Jail.' He wrote it on April 16, 1963. Part of it says,

Injustice anywhere is a threat to justice everywhere. When knowing something is immoral or illegal, and they chose to standby idly — to do nothing in the face of wrong makes one complicit and guilty of aiding or accepting injustices.

"Although your wrongdoing had nothing directly to do with civil rights, you did help violate the store owner's right not to have his property removed without paying for the items."

I hear my dad take a deep breath on the phone before he continues his explanation.

"Marley, a business must raise prices to cover the cost of stolen or damaged property. That makes all of us pay for the wrongs of a few.

You are now part of that few who have a cause and effect on others that you will never know. You helped your friends take something that did not belong to them. They did not see or feel a sense of right and wrong. Your friends should have known how you feel, and you shouldn't have been there. Know this—you will pay the cost in another way.

"Now, hand the phone to your mom, so we can discuss your behavior."

My dad is a Mercedes Benz mechanic, and his dealership sent him to learn a new computer system for new cars in Germany for the summer. We worry about him being in another country and so far away from us. He sends pictures of landmarks that describe tragic aftermaths in a country where they did awful things to people.

Once he finishes, he will come back to train other mechanics at the dealership where he has worked his way up to the position of head mechanic. My dad is a super-smart man. He always tells me the most rational thing he has ever done was to marry my mother and have a son by her. He said that again while we were on the phone, although he's also disappointed with me for disrespecting myself and my family.

My dad is a self-made man, as his friends speak of him. He played football in college, and they say he was an overachiever because of how hard he worked. My dad did not receive a scholarship to play football; he walked on and made the team. Within one year, my dad had made all-conference honors.

I can't keep up with him when we train. Even though he takes it easy on me, I feel like I'm about to pass out when we run or lift weights. My dad is the strongest man I know, but he is also a gentle person and always playful.

But he may not be so cuddly when he comes back this time. Everyday, I'll have to think about my dad making me put in the work of three men, if I have the chance to play basketball in high school.

Chapter 4

I continue to wake from nightmares of my mom and dad telling me how bad my summer is going to be. I go in the bathroom and stare at the mirror. At first, I see myself. Then it's like I'm looking at my mom again, and hearing her stern punishment repeated all over again.

"You are grounded for the whole summer," she said, with a tone that made my stomach bubble.

I'd cocked my head like our dog does and looked at my mother, thinking, *Are you serious?* Then I was apologetic over and over, saying I was sorry.

I hoped to hear, "I should ground you for the next week."

But no. What did she say? "You are grounded for the whole summer. And I mean every day of the summer. Do you hear me, Marley Barton Tingle? Do you understand me?"

Yes, she said my full name.

"I do, Mom."

Now, I'm wide awake at midnight again, curled up on the floor in a corner of my room, feeling sorry for myself. My mom had not let me off the hook.

Before all this went down, I was sure my summer was going to be one of the best. I planned to go to movies with my friends, to see the latest comedy or action flick. I anticipated going to the mall and spending sunny afternoons swimming at the lake.

The prettiest girl I know, Alana Kona-Parks, is my super-close friend, and she and I were going to hang out. She's kind of old school, like me, when it comes to fashions and traditional hip-hop style. She wears her hair in Afro puffs or sometimes a huge afro. She likes handmade jewelry and has a ring on each finger, a lot of bracelets on each wrist, and has a name for each one.

We both like old school hip-hop music. She treats everyone nice and never has a bad thing to say about anyone. Well, not most of the time. Alana can really look at you with her big brown eyes. She always makes me wonder if she is the smartest, sweetest girl in our whole school, as she is cool with most everyone.

Her mom sees me as a close male classmate, almost like I'm her big brother, but we tell others we will date, after our freshman year.

I wanted to walk with Alana around the Pike Place Market this summer. We could watch those big fish be thrown from one person to another, and then ride a ferryboat to Bainbridge Island and return back across Puget Sound at sunset.

Last summer, I went down to the Pike Place Market with my cousin from out of town. He and I hung out, eating freshly made donuts and walking around. I stopped to watch the making of a silver beaded necklace by a Native American woman with a jewelry shop there., and I thought about Alana.

The Native woman seemed to know what was on my mind and asked me whether I was interested in the necklace for my mother or my girlfriend. I told her it was for my mother. But the actual truth is, I wanted to gift Alana. I asked the beader whether I could pay for it a little at a time, until I had paid in full.

"No, son," she said. "It is for a girl. You and she share smiles and dreams. Eyes tell the truth. I will make you two necklaces of two different designs for the same price as for one."

"Two?"

"For you, if you simply tell the truth."

The Native woman handed me a necklace set with the stones in amazing colors.

"Ma'am, I will try to pay you for both. I can't take them from you for nothing. Your art shines, and the stones sparkle."

"It is well within my soul to gift you if you will make womenfolk happy, being the kind of young man you can and will be, if only you tell the truth."

She handed me another necklace with brass bronze and silver.

"I love the different metals, ma'am."

"Then your mother will have one, as well as the young lady who has your eye."

She pointed to the pigeons walking on the ground then lifting to fly short distances closer to the people who were milling around. "In time, I will do what a pigeon, raven, and an eagle do and lift to the sky. Then, I will leave gifts for those I leave behind, to remind them to live for others."

"I don't understand," I told her.

"No matter. But what you must understand as you travel through eternities, young man, is never to use your mother's name in a hollow echo. You must always be honest with a girlfriend, a wife, and a mother, a sister. Let it be *all* women who will hear the truth from you. Things will happen in life that might not be so good, if you mislead a woman. A woman can bring healing to your body. Most of all, a woman can heal a wounded spirit. Son, don't be a liar! Accept responsibility for what you do by being honest."

The Native woman made sense. I understood her to say that even little lies can hurt someone, and they can hurt me, as well. She was direct with me, but she did not use a harsh tone. It was more like a plea. I have been going to the market and making small payments and will have paid in full by next summer.

~✺~

Sadly, my plans to hang out with Alana down at the Market are gone before they even begin. I messed up. I can't even go to the park and play ball.

Ugh! I need to play. I have to be ready to play hoops for high school basketball. My game is good, but I want to be great. Two weeks ago, before school let out, I played in a pre-summer outdoor basketball tournament by the lake, and I was the player of all players on the court. I keep replaying the action from the game...

From the sidelines, I could hear "*Oohs*" and "*Ahs*," as Jamelle and I went at each other, as we always do.

He's going to be a junior at the rival school to where I will be going for high school next fall. Ever since we were kids, we've had it in for each other on the court. He was bigger than me at one time, being a little older, but now we are the same height.

I know I have more game than he does, but he's good. I can't take him lightly, and I don't. We talk a lot of head game on the court, and we play hard. In one of the games, Jamelle crossed me over, but I slapped the ball out of his hand for a steal and headed down the court. He chased me.

I know he was thinking I was going in for a layup, and I knew he hoped to block my shot.

I stopped at the 3-point line and sidestepped, to make sure he couldn't get to me. I pulled up for the shot, and it went in, touching nothing but net.

I heard, "*Oh!*" and "*Ah-ha!*" from all the other players in the game...

Next year, I had hoped to play minutes on varsity, so I have been working out every day. I lift weights, run the track, shoot for an hour or more, and play on the public courts. My game is nice, and my 3-point shooting range would have people in the stands cheering.

But now that I'm grounded for the summer, I can only shoot and run wind sprints in our backyard. At least I have a weight set at home.

Also on my summer agenda, I was going to go to my grandparents' house. My granddad has an old car that he calls a classic. I think it is a 1966 Chevrolet Impala, but whatever it is, it is an oldie, for sure. He lets me help him work on the car and says he'll teach me to drive, if I help him clean and wax his classic. I think he will let me take the car to my senior prom in a few years.

But I messed up. I had places to be and lots of great plans, but now, I've lost my freedom.

Chapter 5

Mom wakes me up early.

"Marley Barton Tingle, take care of these clothes." She drops a load of laundry on my bed for me to iron, fold, and put away. "And here is a list of chores. *Don't* look at the list and ask me why you have to do *anything* on the list. You *know* why."

In disbelief, I read the list of chores over once, twice, three times. It is full of things I have never had to do before.

"Marley Barton Tingle," Mom continues, again saying my full name, since she is *especially* upset with me. "You must be self-disciplined, a self-starter, and finish no matter what is put in front of you. You are a smart young man with much to give. And you have a family, teachers and even some friends who all advocate for you to be your best and shine."

Despite the trouble on my last day of school and my grades, I think my mom and dad are being a bit hard on me. I mean, the *whole* summer? What good is *that* going to do for me? Being grounded for a whole summer is a lot to take in, but I have to get started and try to make the best of it.

After I take care of the whole pile of laundry, I stare out the window into blinding sunshine and daydream about being down at the lake, swimming with my friends. Then, before I know it, I am back to reality, just sitting in my room alone and staring out the window.

I feel embarrassed. How do I tell Alana? Mom said I was allowed to call and tell her I am on restriction for the whole summer, but that might not be enough. Maybe I should ask to go to a new school, so no one there will know I've been grounded for three months. My mom has already said there will be no TV, no cell phone, and no Tik Tok or Instagram until next September.

People who I normally hang around with might really question who I am now, after this punishment, and whether it is cool to have me around. People can be funny when they find out someone did something out of character. They might *think* they know what I did or didn't do.

Truth is, though, it didn't change who I am. I made a mistake, yes. But who doesn't? And I still don't think I did anything all that bad.

Yet, I think, what will Alana's mother think of me. She is like a second mom to me. And what will the coach at my new high school think of me, if he finds out about the kind of trouble I've been in? How will my other friends and classmates feel about me? I sure used to have the image of being someone who is above getting involved in crimes like shoplifting!

Why should I care about what is none of their business?

The next morning, after another night of nightmares and being unable to sleep, Mom threatens to send me to my grandmother's house in Jamaica, for a summer of work picking Spanish limes, mangos, coconuts, and sweet potatoes. I know she wouldn't, as that threat is something she always says, when we act up. Mom even says that to my dad, when he goes motorcycle riding with his friends! She wants to remind him he better not speed and have an accident. My dad laughs at her warnings, but I think he kind of believes her.

I can still shoot hoops in the backyard, but just by myself, and I'm allowed to jog my block back and forth. Other than that, Mom says the only place I can go is to the library, so I plan to go every day, in order to get out of the house. I might even read a book... I'm glad the library has comics.

I plan to do a lot of writing, since I'll have time on my hands. I love to write. I really have no excuse for receiving a bad grade in my language arts class, because writing is easy for me. I just failed to do the work. I have no other excuse.

First, I'll write letters of apology to Alana, to my grandparents in the islands, my grandparents here, and to my mom and dad. Ah, then maybe I'll get off from being grounded. I know my parents love writing.

Reading and writing has been key to how my mother and father made a good life for my siblings and me. We hear that a lot around the house: what is on the paper is how to find a way to a good life.

Chapter 6

The next day, I sit in my room again after doing some chores. It is a hot morning. I can hear my younger sisters playing outside with other kids.

Some of my friends walk by the house, and I hear them knock on the front door. Then, my mom tells them, "Marley cannot come outside. He can't play or hang out with you this summer." I'm so embarrassed.

I think I'm going to go crazy. I head downstairs to the living room, where my mom made me put my laptop, so she can watch all my screen activity. She also gave me a list of historical figures and events she wants me to research while she supervises from nearby.

I start in, doing some research on the list, which includes:

Toussaint Louverture, the leader of the Haitian Revolution.

Shaka Zulu and Sigidi kaSenzangakhona, who was the King of the Zulu Kingdom from 1816 to 1828.

Althea Gibson, an American tennis player and professional golfer; also, one of the first Black athletes to cross the color line of international tennis.

Also on the list is *The Tragedy of Othello, the Moor of Venice,* a play by William Shakespeare. I am supposed to read it to understand its themes of passion, jealousy, and race.

After I do all this, I am supposed to give my mom an oral report. Then she will add other people for me to look up. When I want a break from my mom's homework, the other activity she'll allow is my going to the library.

I go back to doing the chores on Mom's list that she has given me. I clean up the dog poop in the backyard and wash my dog. After I finish vacuuming, Mom says I can go to my room or hang out in the backyard with my dog.

I decide to shoot hoops in the backyard. My friends still can't shoot with me, but it's cool. I focus on my form instead of wasting time. After 500 shots, I hit 400. Then, after I take a shower, I ask to go to the library.

"Marley, the library *only!*" she says.

On my long walk to the library, I think about what has transpired since my friends' shoplifting and me not stealing but being lumped in with them; it makes no sense to me. As I walk past some other friends' houses, kids who were not part of the store escapade, my walk turns into a jog. I rush on quickly, hoping to avoid their teasing, if they have heard about my dilemma.

My sisters, who are in sixth and seventh grade, found out that the parents of my friends who actually shoplifted only yelled at them. No other punishment. This upsets me. I think about telling my mother that it's unfair I'm being grounded for the summer while my friends are out having fun.

But then I think better of talking to her and laugh at my silly thought. No point in piling on a bad situation and making it worse. I already know what my mom would say "I pay the bills in this house, and when you get a job and have your place, you can then make decisions for yourself. But even then, there are consequences."

I keep walking to the library. I wear my favorite, three-toned bowling shoes. My friends mock me for wearing what they call "old man's shoes," but I think they are cool. Tomorrow, I'll wear my running shoes and use the trip back and forth to the library to get in shape. I hope maybe Mom and Dad will let me go to the track at school and start running this summer. I'll offer to take my sisters, because for sure they will put me on blast, if I'm not running and just hanging out with friends while we're there.

Ten blocks later, I pass the same type of store where my friends shoplifted. It reminds me how I'm the one who needs to be a better person and leader and not a follower.

The library is an old brick building with stone steps, huge wooden doors, and tall windows. I show my ID to the librarian, which all kids must do, to visit the library.

The librarian says, "Oh, Marley, I have an email here from your mom. She said no computer time for you. You are allowed to read books and magazines only."

I should have known. My mom is a detailed person and just the type to contact the librarian ahead of my getting there.

I head over to the comic books, and decide I'll read the ones about Black Panther, Spiderman, Aquaman, and Silver Surfer. After a while, though, I get tired of reading comic books and lay my head down on the table to take a nap...

I'm roller skating at the rink. Alana teases me as I almost fall...

Then... I'm playing basketball down at the lake and scoring on everybody. Along the courtside, my friends give me mad props. I'm on a fast break about to dunk the ball and...

I startle awake. It is hot. I have beads of sweat on my neck. If only I were in a cool, air-conditioned movie theater... I wish I was at my grandparents' house, drinking ice-cold tea in the garage with Grandad. I can almost hear his radio loudly playing blues music.

I head to the bottled water dispenser, purchase some water, and sit outside on the steps to get some air. Carlos and Devon roll up on their bikes.

The three of us have known each other since first grade and have done many things together. We went camping with one another's parents, played Little League baseball and football, among other things. And we dress somewhat alike. Devon and I have locs, though mine are longer. Carlos, who is Hispanic and Black, wears his hair curly hair in a wild afro. I'm six-foot two, tall for my age and still growing, while my two friends are both around five-foot seven.

They are smiling, and I'm not.

"Yo, Marley, I saw your mom," Carlos says as he pulls up. "She said you are super-grounded." He stops smiling after he says this. I hope he knows I'm not happy with what he's just said.

"Bro, that's messed up," Devon says, throwing his hands up in the air like he is shooting a basketball and not even looking at me when he talks. "You didn't even take anything. My mom did a lot of hollering and threatened to make me go live with my dad, which would not be that bad for me, and she knows it. Marley, how about we talk to your mother and tell her you didn't do anything?"

"What? So, like, she'll let me hang out with the two who *did* steal? What kind of sense does *that* make? Oh, it doesn't. You guys can't be here talking to me. And I *did* do something wrong. I knew what you guys were doing, and I acted as if it didn't matter. I should have told you guys not to do it. I shouldn't have even been there with you."

We stare at each other for a while.

Then I stand up and head inside the library. "I'm going back inside before I lose the one thing I can do. I guess I'll see you guys when school starts."

Devon calls out, "Hey, Marley, our bad, about how all this came down."

"Yeah, man, sorry." Carlos taps himself over his heart.

I nod and go back inside the library.

Chapter 7

I go to the publication rack and pick up a few sports magazines to take back to the table. I don't read the articles, just look at pictures and read the captions.

Before long, I feel like just chilling and doing nothing. I lay my head on the top of the pile of them like a cushion. I'm not as sleepy as I was before, but I start to daydream, like I usually do before falling asleep. I've even been caught drifting off like this at school, which has caused a few notes to be sent home...

Alana is walking along the lake with me. We stop and turn her phone up loud, to listen to music. We sit on a park bench and stare at the water...

"Marley, imaging having a personal sea-going vessel so we could cross oceans and go places few people ever go."

"I know, right?" I reply. "If we go anywhere, we could see people who look like us but speak different languages. Then, we learn to understand what they say and how to speak to them."

"Yeah. If we could see how others live, we wouldn't judge them by comparing them to what we know. We would learn to adapt to their lifestyle. That is how it should be. Just think, Marley."

"I know, when I have tuned into class and we are doing geomapping, I've noticed how the mountains around the world are different and the oceans bring people different ways to live and earn their money. Sadly, though, we also learned how, throughout history, people have had their resources stolen. The diamond mines in South Africa kept the original Africans living under a sad state of apartheid, because of money the White landowners made from mining.

"When I read about South Africans and how the people were done wrong, like forced to live in shantytowns, it makes me mad. Then there was those who fought for their land so that people could live as they had before, when they were free. Even centuries ago, a warrior named Shaka Zulu tried to free his people from colonial rule, but he could not, in the end. Then along came Nelson Mandela to help free his people."

Marley makes me think about what would happen if we could cross oceans. Maybe we would fly, but either way, if we can go places, we can change things, both inside ourselves and out.

"Alana," I say as we sit by the lake, "here we are, looking out over this big body of water. But a lake is like a drop of rainwater compared to the ocean. Flying or sailing over huge oceans to go places and change bad things would be amazing. If only we could..."

"If you don't read, they will imprison you."

A little short white lady wakens me with this odd words.

I lift my head suddenly. Standing over me is a librarian I have never seen before. It is definitely not Alana from my daydream.

"Huh?"

"Young man, *huh* is not a question," she admonishes, but her voice isn't harsh. "The guttural sound you made is to imply you have a question. So, ask."

I rub my eyes and take a deep breath. "No, ma'am, I do not have a question."

I want to speak respectfully to adults. I never talk back or act rudely to a teacher or anyone older than me. That is how I was raised.

The lady standing next to where I sit in a wooden chair is short, her head barely above mine. She wears a white blouse with ruffles down the center and on the sleeves around her wrists, like ones I have seen on older women in the TV Westerns I watch with my grandparents. Her white hair is tied in a big bun, and she has round-wire-rimmed glasses perched on her nose.

I think she is old. She wears her skirt well below her knees, over thick stockings, and her shoes remind me of tap-dancing shoes. Behind her, is a book cart loaded with lots of books, though I have never seen her at any time before putting books on the shelves.

The lady stares at me a moment and then turns to the book cart, selects a book that she places on the table in front of me, and walks away.

I'm puzzled. I did not ask for a book. I have never come to the library and had a librarian place books on my table before. As she pushes the cart away and turns the corner, her short form vanishes behind a bookcase.

The book she placed on the table is not thick. I pick it up and flip through its pages. It's only a little over a hundred pages long, which is about as much I would want to read. The title is a bit strange: *Animal Farm*, it's called. By George Orwell.

"Young man, it is important to know how the world works. Or should I say how it has worked until now."

I look at the lady as she keeps talking, hoping neither she nor I seem crazy.

"*Animal Farm* is a humorous fantasy, written in 1945," she continues and then tells me about the book with the funny title. "After longing for civil rights and freedom from rule, a group of farm animals revolts against their owner. A pig named Napoleon undermines the elected leadership and becomes a dictator.

"After the animals overthrow the humans, they rename the farm "Animal Farm." They agree with the main rule, that all animals are equal. Napoleon, the main pig, decrees himself the supreme commander-in-chief and elevates the pigs to leadership positions for their personal gain.

"Much like the history of the world, different leadership battles, from communism versus capitalism through the prejudices, intolerances, and the selfish make history repeat as farm animals model human experiences. *Animal Farm* is one of the greatest books of our times."

Then the lady walks away, as if she is leaving me no choice but to read, so I begin to read. And three hours later, I finish the whole thing. It makes me laugh and causes me to think about some of the things we studied in history.

I enjoy the book. At first, the pigs have a good message, but then, they become power-hungry and selfish. The book points out many aspects of human nature.

The book also reminds me of the fact that I do love to read. And it really held my attention.

I look around for the old White lady, as I want to thank her and ask to read more books like this one. But I don't see her. Maybe she is off from work.

Chapter 8

Later that evening, Mom serves dinner on the back deck. She asks, "What did you read at the library?"

I expected her to ask this, because it is her way of learning whether I'm hanging out in the library just to get out of the house. I'm glad I read a book today.

It feels good to tell her about the book *Animal Farm*. I tell her without her asking about the parallels I understood as to how America and Russia compare, when it comes to capitalism versus communism, and dictatorship versus democracy.

I think I impressed my mom, because she lets me call Alana and talk for five minutes. I tell Alana what transpired and how my summer outlook has changed. I apologize for disappointing her and messing up all the plans we made.

I think Alana's feelings are hurt. She tells me she isn't mad at me, but she does not have a lot more to say. Once, while I was hanging out with my grandfather, he mentioned that when someone does not say a lot, it's best not to press the conversation, even if you normally would.

I'm not permitted to watch TV unless it is a family night for watching—yet another restriction for the summer. So, I go to bed early.

I'm up early, too, since I go to bed before midnight. Once I do my chores, I lift weights and then shoot the basketball 500 times.

While I'm shooting, Mom yells out the window, "I need you to work on your schoolwork just as hard as your shot."

This throws me off my game. After making ten shots in a row, I miss the next five.

I work on my dribbling skills after that and then run wind sprints for twenty minutes. I'm glad we have an enlarged backyard. My parents tell me I make it look easy with my speed. Since both parents were once runners, it is easy to push myself, as running comes naturally.

But when it comes to long distance, my mom burns me down to the ground. She claims to have baby fat from having children and she is more than twice my age, but whenever she and I go to Seward Park and run the loop, she leaves me far behind. No matter how hard I try, I can't keep up with her. Then my mom talks smack to remind me she only runs on the full moon. She beats me when we run together, *even though* she only runs once a month!

I shower and ask Mom if I can go to the library. She stares hard at me, which means, "Go directly to the library—no stop-offs!"

I'm wearing my jogging shoes, and I run there with some pace. I have a small backpack filled with some books I need to return for my sister. I also have a towel, bar soap, and deodorant to wash up in the library's bathroom when I get there. I don't want to smell sweaty while sitting inside for hours. I also packed bottled water, some raisins, an apple, and an orange.

As I come out of the library bathroom, I don't see the little old lady pushing around the book cart. I see other librarians but not the little old lady. The library has super-tall ceilings, oak woodwork, and hardwood doors, with windows almost from the floor to the ceiling. Sometimes, they have to close the library down to redo the floors, much like a basketball court. Even with air conditioning, it is still hot inside. But there is an outdoor reading court, and I decide to go out there.

Once I browse the magazine rack and make some selections, I sit in one of the cozy chairs in an area they call the reader's circle. I start to read *High School Top 100 Basketball Report*. As I flip through the pages, I start to imagine myself as one of the top 100 basketball players in the country, playing in front of huge crowds at All-Star Games.

I look up each time someone comes into the library. People walk about or sit at tables with their laptops or books. I see a few kids from my school, but none of them are my friends. Still, we nod at each other.

I reach in my backpack and quietly pull out a little box of raisins, even though no food is allowed. My eyes scan the room to make sure no librarian can see me, then I pour raisins in my hand and munch on a few at a time.

I continue to read and daydream about being on the basketball court. I don't even have to close my eyes. I just look out the window, where the blue sky is like a big-screen TV...

I see myself stealing the ball and dribbling down the court. As I do a crossover dribble past the last defender, I hear the crowd screaming, "Ooohhh." "Sky walking," as my friends call my jumping ability. I dunk on someone who thought they could jump with me...

My daydream is interrupted when I feel eyes on me. I peer over the top of my magazine and see the little old lady librarian at the main desk. She is staring at me through the double doors that lead out to the outside reading area. As I put some raisins in my mouth, she points her finger in my direction and beckons me to come over.

"If you don't read, they will imprison you," she says again, like yesterday.

I stare at her, not wanting to say the wrong thing. I feel stuck and can't move.

"If you don't read, they will imprison you. Do you understand?"

"No, I'm sorry, I do not understand."

"You only read magazines. All reading has value, but books with the accounts of people, places, and past times, given through a narration of printed word, chronicle descriptions and thoughts of people. Reading the books I speak of will teach you to avoid the present and future mistakes. Forgotten, historical events and figures deliver the highest value to your future."

The old White lady is even shorter than I realized yesterday. My sixth-grade sister is five-foot four, and this woman is much shorter. Her head and shoulders are barely visible over the top of the checkout desk where she stands.

She reaches toward me, gesturing for the magazine I hold in my hand. The ruffles on her blouse cuff pull up above her wrist, exposing her forearm. I see a tattoo there—maybe a Bible verse number? My eyes focus on what I think I see. I find it super-odd that an old lady has a tat. I have never seen a tattoo on an actual older adult.

She pulls her sleeve down. I think she caught me staring.

My dad has a couple of tattoos. A few guys in high school have tight tattoos, and, for sure, the pros and rappers have tattoos, but I've never seen one on an older lady before. I do have one teacher who has a tattoo on her ankle, but she's young and new to teaching.

"Ma'am, I don't mean to be disrespectful, but please tell me, is that a tattoo? And if it is, what is it a tattoo of?"

"Young man, hand me that magazine." Her tone is firm, though not mean. But on her face, her eyes are piercing. I don't know if she is mad or just disturbed that I've asked this question.

"Ma'am, am I in trouble?"

She reaches for a book from behind the counter and hands it to me. The Ways of White Folks: Stories, by Langston Hughes. Langston Hughes is a poet I do know of. One student at my school recited his poem, "Weary Blues," at assembly during Black History Month.

"Follow me, please," she says and starts to leave the checkout counter area.

I hesitate, but then she stops and looks back at me as I stand in place.

"Come with me," she says. "And you are not in trouble unless you don't read."

The lady walks past the office with me walking slowly behind her. It is not hard to keep up with her, because of her short legs, but my walk is timid. I don't need more trouble on top of my problems. And I'm not sure what I did wrong. The tone of her voice and the way she said to follow her makes me feel I'm in trouble.

We pass a preschool reading area where young kids and parents are sitting on the floor, listening to an animated presentation by another young librarian. Then, we turn left into a hallway, and she pushes an elevator's down button.

When the door opens, we take it down to where it stops and wait a long time for the door to slowly open. I follow her into a small corridor that connects to other hallways and rooms that are filled with racks loaded with lots of books. They appear different than the ones upstairs. Most of these books are old and have hardcovers. The spines don't have a lot of colors.

I follow her to a sign over a rack that reads:

Once she stops, she reaches for a book, but it is too high up on the shelf for her. "Young sir, please, the book with the faded red spine. Please pull that one down."

I reach up, watching her, until I touch the book she's requested. Then I remove it from the upper shelf and hand it to her.

We head over to a table, and she signals for me to sit. The lady sits across from me.

"This is an old book from a period long ago. It is a hardback first edition. There are plenty of editions of this book in paperback, but I would be grateful if you could hold this aged book. While you read this true story, you will feel, see, and be in another time. It will seem as though you are going back in time."

I look at the faded lettering on the old book. The title reads, *The Diary of a Young Girl.*

"You are welcome to read this edition down here," she adds. "In this reading room. I cannot check this book out to you, but upstairs, you can check out a paperback version for you to read."

A few things enter my mind. First, it is cool down here in the basement, so different from how hot it is upstairs. I had been nervous, thinking maybe I was in trouble, but the lady is kind of chill.

Next, I want to know why she wants me to read this book. It is much thicker than the *Animal Farm* book. No way I'll be able to read this book in just a few hours. But I decide to check out the paperback version to take home and then to come back here to the library and continue to read the old edition. I feel something inside when I hold the old book.

Now that she has said more than the few words, the old lady does not seem as odd to me as I'd thought, after our first interaction.

Once we are upstairs again, we walk out of the slow elevator and find ourselves back into the heat. The old librarian tells me on what shelf I can find the book's paperback version. She explains it will have a different title, and it will be *The Diary of Anne Frank*.

The last thing she says is, "They will imprison you if you do not read." Then she disappears around the corner.

I want to ask why she keeps repeating that negative and maybe harsh thought. But I asked one question already today, so I decide to go look for the book.

When I find it, the first thing I do is read the back cover.

A young girl, Anne Frank, while hiding for two years with her family during the Nazi occupation of the Netherlands, kept a diary. Apprehended in 1944, Anne Frank died of typhus in the Bergen-Belsen concentration camp in 1945. Now, the book has been published in more than 70 languages since 1942. The popularity inspired the 1955 play, The Diary of Anne Frank, *and was then adapted for a movie in 1959. Many awards presenters list the book as one of the best of the twentieth century.*

I check the book out and go back to where I was sitting, still perplexed about my interaction with the old librarian. My grandmother has told me several times that, in life, we can meet someone for just five minutes and their impact can be as important or more than someone we may know a lifetime.

I feel a bit rattled, as if I was on the foul line in a basketball game and might miss a free throw. I put the book in my backpack and leave the library. Going home, I jog with more pace than ever before. When I reach our house, I'm pouring sweat. I say, "Hi, Mom," and head upstairs.

From behind me, I hear, "You weren't gone long." Mom's tone is questioning.

"I checked a book out and thought I'd come home and read.

"You checked out a book?"

"Yes, Mom." I wait for her to say something else or ask another question. When I don't hear one, I shower and head to the kitchen. I pour a glass of juice and sit with the book on the back deck instead of my bedroom.

Underneath the shade umbrella, I start to read. In 1942, Anne Frank was the same age that I am now. She was born and lived where my father is right now, in Frankfurt, Germany. I think about my dad over in Germany for work.

Anne Frank describes moving to Holland after an evil man named Hitler came to power in her country. Anne and her family were Jewish. They fled Germany when the Nazis put the Jewish people under harsh, unfair treatment. Unfortunately, the Germans next took over Holland, and the rules for Jewish people there were awful.

The rules for Anne and her family were extremely difficult, and I wondered whether I could live under the same rules. The Jewish people had to wear a yellow star to identify themselves from others. Anne and all Jews were not allowed to ride bicycles. Anne watched a German policeman ride her bike when she left it out front, making her sad. I would have been angry.

There was a law that Jewish people could not drive cars and were not allowed on trains. Her mother and father could only shop in Jewish shops for a couple of hours each day and then had to stay indoors after 8:00 p.m.

While reading her story, the horrors reminded me of what we learned about America's history of segregation and lack of civil rights for Black, Native American, and Asian people. The Nazis forced Jews into Jewish-only schools. Jews could not go to the movies or stage plays or watch sports, and could not have friends of other religions.

I have a few Jewish friends, but I never knew their people went through an awful period in history like many other races such as my own. America enslaved Black people for nearly 400 years.

The sun on our rear deck can become intense. I go into the house to take a break once I am pretty far along in the book. I read fast when I read, and my teachers tell me I have high comprehension skills, meaning I understand at a higher level than most, retaining what I read.

My mom is in the kitchen, cutting onions. My eyes start to water before I've been in the kitchen for even a full minute. I pour some juice while my mom talks on the phone to my grandmother. She is not shedding one tear, but I have to try not to rub my burning eyes from the cut onions.

"Here, talk to your grandmother. Stay in the kitchen."

I know mom thinks she's being funny, knowing my eyes are tearing from onions. She does this to us kids all the time.

"Young man, I'm upset with you because of your behavior."

My grandmother has the sweetest voice, but I hear something in her voice that makes my stomach feel weird. I'm sad because my grandmother loves me as no one else ever will. I knew my grandparents would hear about what I did, and I hurt for them. I want to be angry with my mother, but she is not the one who did what I did.

"Marley, I will talk to you later, okay" she says. "I need to finish talking to your mother. But you call me."

"Yes, ma'am."

I wait back out on the deck for my mother to finish talking on the phone. Then I ask, "Mom, may I go on YouTube to see what I can find out about Anne Frank?"

"Why?"

"I'm reading a book about her."

"Okay. But only look up that subject for now. And thank you for asking. It lets me know you may be taking your restriction seriously."

After I type *Anne Frank* into the computer, it takes less than a second before non-stop videos and even a full-length movie shows up. I click on a movie clip, and it seems to show a visual of what I've read so far in the book. There is a dreary, bleak background, but the girl who portrays Anne has a cheerful outlook, even though she has to stay inside the place she and her family moved into. Their life seems pretty small when they are in hiding.

I decide maybe I should finish reading the book before I watch the full feature film. I turn the movie off and watch some commentaries. After a while, I feel a bit sleepy and go up to my room to lie down and take a nap.

When I awake, it seems like I have been dreaming in black and white, with only bits and pieces in color. I remember picturing a young White girl looking out a window and not being able to go outside and play. She watches someone in a military uniform riding her bicycle, and it makes her feel sad.

Chapter 9

I wait until later in the evening to talk to my G-mommy. She is the sweetest woman on Earth, and it hurts me that her grandson let her down. She is always bragging about me to all her friends and other family members, when we have reunions.

"G-mommy, I know I let you down. I'll work harder on my grades. I'll take going to school more seriously, and I'll be more mindful of what my friends might be doing."

"Marley, my usually sweet grandson, you are still my shining star. I know, one day, you will bring pride to all who know you. You know, I made plenty of mistakes. I don't want you to think I was perfect. It was a while ago when I did things I regret. I do know it would be best if you learned to think before letting your actions or words hurt yourself and others. Some things can stay with us for a long time. You will overcome this time in your life. You will live up to the promise of a good life full of good deeds.

"I will ask your mother to let you spend a day here and there with your grandfather and me, but you can't treat what happened as if you are getting away from being grounded. And, Marley I'm not sure you understand, it is not about watching what your friends are doing.

That is one of the reasons you are having a summer like you are. You were part of the crime. If you had the slightest idea something was going on, you helped them steal. Did y'all share your candy?"

I could not get a word to come out. I was on the phone, feeling stuck.

"Marley, answer me."

"Yes, G-mommy."

"Okay. Let's change the subject."

"Okay." I felt my heart pumping again, as if it had stopped while she was speaking. I love my grandmother and don't want her to be mad at me for anything. "I want to tell you I am reading a book. It's called *The Diary of Anne Frank*."

"Marley, I'm glad to know you are reading. I read that book in the 1960s, before your mother and father were born. And I have watched the movie a few times."

"I was going to watch the movie, too, G-mommy, but decided to finish reading the book first. Maybe, when I finish reading the book, we can watch the movie together. I'm sure you can point out some things for me to understand even more."

"Yes. But keep reading. The best way to learn more background about what you will watch later is to read a book. You will learn about the loss of freedoms or never having civil rights."

I ask, "But how can one group can be evil to another group of people, using lies and deceptions to control them? The Nazis eliminated a great number of Jews and in horrible ways."

She explains, "Black people in America and in the Islands know about these repressions all too well, as the wrongs have happened here in different forms for 400 years."

"History has never been my best subject in school," I admit. "But the librarian, in a strange way, has encouraged me to read this book, and I think it's cool to read about someone my age who went through tough times."

"History will guide you to avoid mistakes and be aware of what is happening around you. People tend to avoid history as a boring subject, which is one of the problems we have in our world. We dislike looking back, as some feel guilty for something they did not do and become insecure about being unaware, so they often deflect. All this leads to a self-inflicted ignorance about the past. People become self-absorbed and limit what they will allow to be put in their head and what others should see or read."

"I never thought about that."

"Marley, please do. Always. It will help you in life to be better and more helpful to the world you will live in."

Chapter 10

Ido my morning chores. Then I do what I can as far as working out in the backyard, lifting weights in the basement, and getting ready to go to the library. I want to continue reading *The Diary of Ann Frank* in the old leather-bound version down in the library's basement.

I was up late night reading the paperback. I stopped when I was too sleepy to go on reading. I was at the point when the family had to hide all the time and was living in a contained space in an upper room of the house. Anne and her family hid out of fear of being sent to concentration work camps.

Jews were the main people targeted for arrest and then sent to those work camps. The Franks had heard that many people had died there. Originally, many Jews might not have believed all they had read or maybe they chose not to read the news reports. But now, they did believe.

This made me think about what the old librarian had been saying to me. "If you don't read, they will imprison you."

"Mom, I am going to the library, okay?"

"Are you asking?" she says in response.

"Sorry, Mom. Can I go to the library?"

"I have seen you reading a book and asking questions. That is good, Marely. So, this is what I have done for you. I called the rec center and spoke to someone about you coming in alone, when no one else is in the gym. You will be allowed to shoot the ball there for an hour."

I almost jump over the table to the other side to hug my mom. She is a big-time hugger and always kisses me on the cheek to embarrass me in front of my friends. I know she does it on purpose. Now, I do it to her, but no one sees me, so I don't care.

"Mom, I love you."

"Oh, did you still love me when I put your butt on restriction, which you are still on?"

"Mom, yes, I still love you." I drop my eyes downward, uncomfortable in my skin for her calling me out.

"No playing hoops with anyone or hanging out," she reiterates. "And I mean it! Oh, you can thank your dad for this."

"Okay," I say, almost running out the door with my ball in the same breath. "Mom, thanks."

She gives me a look meant to say, "Don't mess up."

I'd rather she yelled at me rather than give me the super-serious mom look. It can make me stop in mid-step, mid-sentence, or wake me out of deep sleep.

⁓❦⁓

Ah, to be on a full-size court, shooting at the hoop! It is really inspiring. I get into my dribbling drills and let my imagination flow, as if I'm in a game.

I throw the ball off the backboard on one end for a rebound, weave up the court with the ball, and do my sweet crossover, as if I am on a fast break. Then, I pass the ball off another wall and act as if I am catching and shooting.

I'm dripping sweat. After an hour, I go to the locker room and shower then change my shirt and shorts. When I arrive at the library, I sit outside on the park bench to soak up the warm sun and take a physical break from the hard work at the gym. I feel like I want to take a nap.

⁂

I stand in the middle of the library, looking for the little librarian. I'm still wondering about her tattoo. I look forward to going into the basement and continuing to read *The Diary of Anne Frank,* but I don't see her anywhere to take me.

I walk over by the elevator next to the steps that lead down into the basement. The elevator opens slowly, and there she is.

"Have you been reading about Miss Anne Frank?" she asks.

I want to impress the little old librarian. "Yes, I have," I say proudly. "And I'm enjoying while learning."

"Take the stair down, and I will meet you."

I nod and head down before the door closes. I work out by skipping several steps at full speed as a leg exercise, keeping my balance with my knees bent and on the balls of my feet. I'm down the two flights of stairs in less than ten seconds, and she is waiting for me. How did the slow elevator beat me?

She walks with me to where the old leather-bound version of *Anne Frank* sits high on the shelf. She points, and I reach for the book. Then, we walk to a small room with one bright light over a table and a chair at each end.

"When you're done reading, I'll be back." Her eyes look dark, and her facial expression makes me want to ask questions, but asking questions is something I think I'll hold off for now. Until I'm done...

"Ah, okay. Yes, ma'am."

She leaves, and I sit facing a small window that looks out into the hallway. The walls in my room are white painted brick. The old book's pages are yellowed, and the lettering looks like one of those old mechanical typewriters.

In the quiet, I flip through the pages, looking for where I left off last night. I think I am the only person down in the basement.

Last night, what I read about the Franks seemed to be what I understand the librarian is saying to me, when she repeats, "If you don't read, they will imprison you." When my mom was a young girl, she says, she heard the phrase, "A mind is a terrible thing to waste."

Maybe the librarian is giving me insight into how I can protect my future. If I read, I could avoid history repeating itself, whether in a particular situation in life or for a group of people. The Jews were hearing Hitler's hateful, destructive, hostile words about what he wanted to do to their race.

Might the Jews have fled, as a people, in order to avoid eventually hiding or trying to escape after it was too late for many of there? Maybe there was nothing the Jews could have done... But should the Jewish people have expected other countries to step up and stop Hitler, before he got started?

No doubt they should have, in my opinion. Every government that was aware of what was going on in Europe at the time and that had the resources to help should have provided the Jewish people a Harriet Tubman-like freedom railroad out of Germany and Poland and Holland and Hungary. Not an underground railroad of hiding out. I assume the Jewish people hoped the world would stand up to the bully and make Hitler do the right things or let him know there would be consequences.

Hitler said that he and the Germans, the Aryan race, were members of the master race. In speeches and newspapers, Hitler declared he wanted more land and separation from non-Aryans so that members of his master race would have ample living spaces. It was clear from all he said and wrote. It was in print, how Hitler intended to expand Germany's boundaries and take land from Poland, Czechoslovakia, Russia, France, and other countries. Hitler declared that Germany's problems were the fault of Jews and dark-skinned people. He considered different populations to be inferior and fit only to serve what he called his master race. He wanted to exterminate entire groups of people.

These were all things I read about. This idea had to be what the librarian was telling me: that, if I don't read, things can happen. I should or might want to be aware and take action to protect myself.

Maybe there is nothing anyone can do, if they believe someone is just being a bully with their words. Maybe having limited resources makes it harder to fight back or move away, before the bully's actual words turn into hateful actions. Can history be changed? I'm left wondering why other countries stood by, back then in Hitler's time, until they were forced to save the world from an evil man. I wasn't alive then, but I still wonder whether we could let another man dictate this kind of evil again.

I assume the German soldiers knew right from wrong. Why didn't they stand up against evil and do the right thing? Did all the German soldiers feel good about following Hitler's orders? Did they want to stand for right? How many wanted to stop Hitler? Half of them? Maybe a quarter of the soldiers? Or was it hardly any? Were they truly indifferent about the plight of the Jews?

I wonder about the Southern Confederate soldiers and how they felt in their conscience, knowing the physical and mental tortures placed upon enslaved. Did they ever feel the pain of the day-to-day lives of enslaved people? How many Confederate soldiers followed orders to avoid firing squads but wanted to end slavery? Or were they indifferent, just shrugging their shoulders?

Maybe, when my friends went into the store and stole, there was nothing I could have done. They might have done whatever they wanted to do, even if I'd protested. But I had knowledge that my friends were stealing. I can't read this and ask why didn't the German soldiers not speak up about any wrongdoing while, at the same time, ignoring my own responsibility in the situation. I must own it. I believe I knew my friend were doing something wrong.

I thought it had nothing to do with me, since I was not the one stealing.

Yet, when I ignored what happened, it did affect me and my well-being. If I had not gone with them, I could have avoided that outcome and spared my parents hurt. Yet, I was there, and I did not do the right thing to step up and attempt to stop them.

❦

I read in the old leather-bound copy of my book how some Nazis entered the house where Anne and her family were hiding. The Nazis had been there several times before. Anne Frank describes how she knew the Nazis knew that Jewish people were hiding in places around the city.

Nazis came by Dutch houses to send warnings to the people of Holland. This was frightening, as Anne Frank and her family had already fled from Germany in an attempt to escape Nazi persecution.

I wish I had taken a nap before going down to the basement, because I feel tired. I am tired. So, I place my head down and use the old book as an odd pillow...

Behind my closed eyes, I see a vision of Alana. She always places herself inside my school locker as I stand there, talking to her. She peers through the slats of the locker, and I can see her eyes. Alana has big pretty eyes, but when she affixes her gaze on me, they always appear to be full of questions.

When I open the locker to let her out, we always have a brother-sister-type hug. Others tease us about it, as if there is more to our friendship. There isn't, though. Not now. But maybe later, in our high school life...

Oh, no... No, no, no...

The room is spinning. It rotates as the room is whirls around like a ball going through a hoop for a swish. I fall out of my chair. I hit my head on the floor.

"*Ouch!*" I say, but only the walls hear me.

My eyes can't focus. My stomach is burbling. Everything I can see is going in different directions from everything else. Then, like the revolving ball that spins and swishes before bouncing on the ground and rolling slowly away, I'm moving around on the floor...

Everything is still cold. It smells a bit musty, but I also smell freshly baked bread.

I am standing in a gloomy room, wearing heavy wool pants. They itch. And the shirt I'm wearing feels heavy. I realize I'm in a uniform with a bunch of buttons down the front.

I see I'm wearing big, heavy, leather boots that shine. But my feet itch, too, like I have wool camping socks on my feet and just stepped out of a cold stream.

There are several people standing in the room with me. I look out a window and see men dressed like me talking to one another.

I feel myself turning my head when I'm not trying to. There is a small mirror on the wall beside some hanging coats. I want to scream, but I can't.

I try to run out the door, but I'm barred from doing what I feel I want and need to do. I see someone other than me in a mirror, but *I'm here, right?* And *why*?

My body won't do what I tell my legs to do. And where would I run? I don't even know where I am, and this is no dream. If this were a nightmare, at least I would know I could wake up, and it would be over.

In the mirror, my face is not my face. My eyes and nose, my full lips and dark skin tone are gone... This person I see is *not* me. It is a young white man! I have pimples and blond hair on the side of my head, and I wear a military hat on top of my head.

I'm flooded with fear. How can this be... *me*? There are two of me. One is standing here as a Nazi, helping to terrorize people, and the other is inside this strange body, with no control. I want to stop the madness. I want to protest the evil around me.

A flag for the Hitler Youth is on my shirt. There is a Gestapo flag is on my coat sleeve. I'm a German. Well, I look the part! But! I'm a Black kid who lives in Seattle and is about to go into high school. How am I inside the body of a young German soldier?

Here I am, part of the secret police force of Nazi Germany. How could this be? Am I dreaming and can't wake from my bad dream? The German Gestapo's ruthless roundup of Jews for deportation to extermination camps is one of history's worst deeds.

I see a man who must be in charge. This head Nazi has power over me. I guess he is a sergeant or something, and he is now yelling at me. He is a Nazi dressed like me but with badges and stripes on the shoulders of his coat.

He speaks loudly to me. "Search this house now, do you hear me? You look everywhere, and you move anything you deem necessary. If there appears to be food that shouldn't be here, I want it noted."

The head Nazi turns from me and points for me to move. He suddenly becomes mean and swings what looks like a miniature baseball bat, knocking a glass bowl off a mantel below a mirror. The glass bowl is beautiful. I think they call the glass a crystal bowl, just like the one my grandmother has. Immediately, the people in the room jump from fear. The people who live legally in the house are in danger, because Anne Frank and her family and others hide in this house.

I want to break free and stop the head Nazi from being evil.

I can't break free.

I'm doing as told.

I wonder, do any Nazi soldiers want to fight against the evil regime I'm immersed in? Or do we all feel helpless?

My boots step on the broken glass, and I hear it crunch under my weight. I'm six-foot two and weigh 160 pounds normally, but in this form where I'm being another man, I must be 200 pounds and five-foot eight.

I move into the action as ordered. I don't want to, but I start looking.

I move about the space and wonder what is going on. I was just inside a room in the basement of my library, reading the book by Anne Frank. Last night, I watched videos about the Nazis and what the Jewish people suffered during World War II.

But I know Anne is in *this* house.

What am I to do? I can't stop my body from searching for her as I head upstairs. I have no control. My mind says *no!* Stop what I am doing. But my body is doing as ordered. I search by moving furniture, lifting rugs, and peering inside closets.

48 | Alvin L.A. Horn

I lie down on the floor and look through a vent.

Oh, no! Eyes appear. They belong to a young girl.

These eyes show fear. Slow tears trickle down cheeks.

Her eyes are beautiful behind the vent.

Her wide but wet eyes beg.

I know what she is thinking.

She is pleading for mercy.

Her eyes say, "Please, don't turn us in."

Then, I finally feel my mouth open, and words come out. I have been trying to talk ever since I found myself inside another person's body.

"Anne, you are safe," I say. "You have nothing to fear from me..."

Oh no! I must look like a rag doll thrown off a cliff, bouncing about uncontrollably as I hit every rock. Or that is how I feel. My eyes can't focus again, and my stomach is waffling.

I crawl around on the floor, trying to get back into my chair, back to where I was sitting before whatever happened began. I'm scared I may have knocked the old book onto the floor and damaged it.

But the book is there on the table, as it was, and the room looks undisrupted. Only I am troubled, my breathing labored. I stand up, but I don't feel stable. I'm sweating as if I've just run miles in dry heat. My mouth is dry, and I need water.

Just then, the little old librarian opens the door. As I turn to look at her, I feel something crunch under my shoe. I lift my foot and step back. There are tiny shards of broken glass, like from the crystal bowl that head Nazi smashed. For the second time in a week, I'm on the floor beside fractured glass.

Wait! *Was I dreaming—a vivid fantasy*? How could there be broken glass under my shoe from a dream?

"Young sir are you done reading for the day?" the librarian asks from the doorway.

"Yes, ma'am. But may I have a broom? There is broken glass on the floor."

"You never mind. Let us head upstairs."

She has me place the old book back on the shelf. As I do, I feel like the floor might be tilted. My eyes can't quite focus... Maybe I'm feeling the pace of time. Something feels off.

I look at the little old librarian, and her face is calm, as if nothing has happened.

Chapter 11

I walk home, reading as I walk. I'm turning pages of my paperback of *The Diary of Anne Frank* as I go into the house. Mom meets me at the door, headed out to water her garden.

"Marley Barton Tingle, you need a shower. You smell like the sweat from crawling out of a mango grove."

"It's this book, Mom! It is so intense."

She places her hand behind my neck and pulls me to her to kiss my forehead. "History can be odd and spellbinding, when we visit someone else's life. Now go on and take a shower and then a nap."

I shower then lie on my bed a start to read again. I read until dinner time, and then I read afterward, until I finish *The Diary of Anne Frank*. When she began writing, she was thirteen years of age, same as I am now, and she was fifteen when she wrote her last entry. She kept up a good spirit as she described her life, including light-hearted passages of her liking a boy and flirting for fun.

The postscript information at the back of the book, after she stopped her journaling, indicates Anne and her family were found hiding in that house and then taken to a Nazi concentration camp. Only her father survived the horrific evils.

A shiver goes through my whole body for her and me. I'm not sure what happened in that room today. I did not dream it—the glass, the crystal pieces on the floor of the room, traveled back with me from 1942. I was inside a young German soldier there, and I did not turn Anne Frank in, although the young Nazi had orders to search the house and destroy lives. My soul overruled they duties, in the end, but a time came later, when I could not save Anne Frank.

I wonder whether maybe the room in the library's basement is paranormally possessed... Did I have an out-of-body experience that took me on an unmagical ride to the past?

Was it the book that sent me back in time?

Or was it my mind?

What if I could have saved Anne Frank?

I did tell her I would not be the one to turn her in.

What more could I have done in 1942?

I'll think about it for a long while.

Chapter 12

I don't sleep well and wake up in the middle of the night. I feel confused. Mystified.

I am out of bed before the sun comes up. I dream with my eyes wide open as I look out my window. I see what happened as if it was a movie before I can shake myself out of my daydream.

I *know* what transpired was no dream. The broken crystal glass proves it was real.

I feel like I tried to do something right to change history. I know I stood up for the right thing, but now I know my best was not good enough.

If I had done the right thing when my friends were doing something wrong, I realize I might have changed history for the better of everyone. The immoral side of history puts people in a constant struggle, even years, decades, and centuries later.

I go downstairs from my room at the same time my mom is having a cup of coffee and doing her morning meditation. She looks shocked to see me.

"Why are you so up so early?"

"I just couldn't sleep.

"Is there anything wrong, besides the fact that you're grounded?"

"No, ma'am. I'm okay."

"All right, well, do your chores, and then I'll let you go to the gym and work out again. If you practice hard enough, maybe you'll tire yourself out and sleep better. Remember—only you in the gym by yourself. Then, you can go to the library."

I think about what the Native woman told me about being honest with my mother. If I say to her there is no problem, *that* could be a problem…

"Mom, I had a rough experience while reading about Anne Frank. It took me places I would never want to be."

"Son, we all have places to be where we only stay for a short while, and then we move on, learn, and grow. We elevate into different spaces and times during our lives. You are up early enough, so call your dad. He should be off work—Germany is eight hours ahead."

"Yes, Mom."

"Hey, Dad," I say when he picks up. "How are you?"

"I'm studying hard over here, son, so I can pass a master's certification on the new computers they are putting in the cars. Then, I can program them. So, I have to say, my eyes are a bit weary from reading."

"I read a good book. I finished *The Diary of Anne Frank*, and I wish I could have saved her. She was a nice and funny girl, and Anne was the same age as me. It was not fair what happened to her."

My sister walks by and says, "Don't hog the phone! I want to talk to Dad."

I ignore her, but she stops and gives me a stare, refusing to stop. "Okay, okay," I tell her. "Give me a minute to talk to Dad. After all, I'm the one who called."

She finally walks away, but not until she gives me a crazy look over her shoulder.

"Dad, the womenfolk around here, as Grandad would say, will not give me a moment of peace." I hear my dad laugh loudly. When he laughs it seems to come from deep within him.

"Son, it is a good thing if a woman seeks your attention. My daughters miss me, too. Maybe more than you. They are younger, and when I am away, it is harder on them."

"I get it. Anyway, about that famous book. I think everyone should read it. The world has often not come to the rescue of those who should never have been in harm's way. Therefore, young man, history is essential. I now know I need to bring you over here and take you to Amsterdam in the Netherlands, to see where Anne Frank lived, the house where she hid."

When he says that, my stomach flips like I'm on a roller coaster. And I feel a slight trembling going through my body, as if I might fall. The house dad speaks of— I was *there*, in a way.

"Dad, please tell me more."

"One needs to understand where we all stand. Imagine you're at the zoo, looking through the window of whatever animal exhibit. You observe behaviors. You notice how animals sleep, eat, and how they communicate. The animal knows you are looking at them. They may do foul or disgusting things because you are watching. You realize they're caged, and you feel happy to be on the right side of the glass. You might feel bad for the animal, but you still know it is far better for you to be on the side of the glass with freedom."

"Dad, when I read about different times, and even now when I watch the news, I find it difficult to understand that some people treat cats, rats, and other animals better than other humans."

"Yes, but you want to be on the right side of the glass in life no matter what. If you conduct yourself negatively or let something bad happen that is well within your control, you'll find yourself on the wrong side of the glass, and your behavior will be the focal point of disrespect.

"I'm here in Germany, a beautiful country, of landmarks of great European history, but even decades after the end of World War II, the people here struggle with having played a significant negative role in history, of being on the wrong side of the glass. Despite all our greatness and achievements, our own country still struggles with a past, too.

"I want you and your sisters to find ways of healing, and how to be the change needed. When we turn a blind eye, it leads to those 'what went wrong' moments in history.

"Your mother has let me know you are doing your chores and reading with a purpose, which is good. But we, as your parents, have never asked you to do anything you don't need to do. Everything we require of you is for your future greatness. With that in mind, your mother and I will soon reevaluate how we feel about your restriction status."

An hour later, I'm on a call with Alana. Dad and Mom have rethought their position and chosen to lift some of the restrictions. They will allow me some activities, and one of them is to talk to Alana. They decided that it was unfair for her, as my best friend, to have her summer upset by my actions.

Her mom has requested for me to take Alana places, so she will feel safe. My parents see something in me I didn't see in myself, which is what elders do. My grandmother said that to me one day.

A little while after that, Alana and I are sitting on the deck in the backyard of my house.

"It is so cool my mom went to pick you up from your house and brought you over here to visit me," I say. "I have been feeling really lonely, with no personal contact with anyone I would want to be around. I do have my sisters, of course, and they've been hanging with me pretty tight, I think because they feel sorry for me." We start laughing hard. Boy, have I been missing moments like this.

"Yeah, Mama Tingle knew I wanted to hang out with you. She said I could come over a couple of days ago, but I couldn't tell you until now."

I look at Alana, and the bright sun is highlighting her. Her beauty is truly in her inner goodness of being my friend and someone I can trust. She is always honest with me. I see what the Native woman meant at Pike Place Market. She told me about always being honest with a woman, and I want to be that man.

"Your parents know they need someone looking out for you," she says.

"Oh, wow, okay. So that is why my mom came and picked you up? But remember, your mom always tells me to watch out for you."

We laugh, and she playfully hits me on the arm. "Tag—got you."

We tap each other on the arm back and forth.

My mom is doing her mom thing, checking in on us. She walks out from the kitchen and gives us the playful eye of "I see you two," as she places two iced glasses of fresh-squeezed mango juice on the table. Then she asks if we need anything else. Mom is big on hosting and treating guests well. I'll hear later about how I did not come inside first and retrieve Alana something to drink.

"Mom, I saw a pretty woman like you, and I just lost my head and forgot to come in and get something for Alana."

"Son, try that line on a pigeon on a wire and watch it just about fall off from hearing the silliness of a foolish boy who thinks he is slick."

We both say, "No, ma'am." We don't need anything else. Then, we wait until she goes back inside. I know my mom trusts Alana and me, but she'll still check on us.

"So, the Pike Place Market can happen?" she asks after a long sip of her juice.

"Yes and no. I'm still on restriction, so I have to keep showing I'm trustworthy."

"Marley, I was mad at you. I was really unhappy when I found out what happened. Please tell me you know it was not cool to be around your homies or home gurls', Carlos, Devon, Sheva, and A-Mm or whatever she calls herself. Not when they may get you in trouble."

"Homies and home gurls'? I'm going to act as if you didn't say that." I take her drink and place it on the other side of me. "You can't have my mom's sweet mango juice. And, since being on restriction, I have been reading books at the library that have me rethinking some things, so I am good."

"If you don't give me my juice, I'll get you in more trouble than your home gurls ever will."

I play like I'm going to give her the drink back a few times before I finally give it to her.

"Whatever you are doing at home to make your mom and dad think better of you, please keep doing it."

"Alana, let me ask you a crazy question." I don't want to tell Alana what happened to me while reading the old book in the library's basement. She might think I'm crazy. So, I decide to ask her some other, less specific questions, just to see if it might be possible for her to understand my strange experience. "Do you believe in time travel?"

"What do you mean, time travel? Like in a science fiction movie, where someone or a group of people move forward or back through time? What was that old movie called?"

"*Back to the Future*."

"Yeah. That was a funny movie."

"For real. My mom and dad rewatch it every time it comes on."

"Is that what you mean when you ask if I believe in time travel?"

"Ah, yeah, that would fit, I guess. I think maybe in my dreams I have time traveled."

"I hope you don't get lost and can't make your way back." Alana laughs, and I laugh with her. "I think your mind is messing with you, and you have some strange memories of floating through deep space."

Alana cracks up as she sits next to me. I laugh with her but, in a sense, not really. Anything makes sense to me when it comes to the time trip I went on. And I know it has nothing to do with memories gone amiss.

When I think about it, I do remember many things that some people might not consider all that important, but the memories mean the world to me. Like I remember my dad picking me up as a toddler, because my little legs were tired at three years of age, when we were walking in a park. I remember dropping my ice cream cone at the zoo when I was five years old. I remember the first time I played in an organized basketball game and the first basket I scored. My memory is clear about what a memory is and is not.

Then... oh no! I feel my chair trembling. I'm about to shake onto the deck floor.

Just as quickly, it stops. The shaking stops.

"Alana, did you feel that?"

"Feel what? I feel a nice breeze in this hot weather. That is all I feel."

Chapter 13

Today, I sit at the computer in the den. I asked my mom could I look up Toussaint Louverture, and she was pleased I had asked. My dad's great-grandfather migrated from Haiti to live in Jamaica. We understand that Toussaint Louverture was a first cousin to my dad's great-grandfather. The formerly enslaved became a general in the Haitian Revolution for Haiti.

I discover documentaries online about how Louverture fought the French, and then, in a strange twist, how he fought with the French, but finally fought France again for Haitian independence. Louverture used his noble leadership wartime skills to bring a revolutionary movement, and he became known as the Father of Haiti, the Black Liberator.

"Mom, may I go to the gym and work out?"

She replies, "I will do you one better. But understand, this is about building trust."

I stand there, silent, unsure what my mom is about to say.

"The high school coach, Coach Barker, called. He and I talked about your situation. He said, if I let you come to open gym with the varsity and JV players in summer scrimmages, he will make you do extra running. He does not want you on the team, if you behave as you did at the end of the school year. He does not play when it comes to bad or average grades. Your father and I will not tolerate you having anything less than a B average. So, with that, young man, I will let you go to the school and practice with the team. Afterward, you can go to the library and keep up what you have started by reading about history."

I run up to my mom and hug her really hard.

"Boy, let go of me before you hurt your mom." She laughs. "Now, you are still grounded, and you cannot hang out or go any other place. Are we clear?"

"Yes, Mom." I sprint upstairs, grab my basketball gear, and run back downstairs. "Mom, how am I going to get to the school? I know open gym is at noon, and it is too late to catch the bus."

"Are you asking for a ride? Because you have a strange way of asking..."

"Mom, will you take up to the school, please? I'll catch the bus from there to the library and walk home after I leave."

Mom picks up her purse and keys. Twenty minutes later, she drops me off at the school. Some varsity players are hanging out in front of the gym.

"Hey, freshman, I know you don't think you are getting any of our playing time." They shout and laugh as I walk past them to go inside the gym.

"Hey, freshman, catch."

Out of the corner my eye, I see a basketball coming toward my head. I stick my arm out and knock it down and then go into a fast dribble, going back and forth, using both hands to do some slick moves. Then I pass it back to the group in what seems like an all-in-one motion, as I keep walking inside.

My dad says people will always try to see what you are made of, if they don't know you. He also says it is their insecurity showing.

Inside, as I walk toward Coach Barker, a few players stretch and do light jogging, while others shoot or goof around. Coach Barker is about six-foot nine and wide enough, I think he has a problem going through some doorways.

"Marley Tingle," he says to me, as he looks downward at me with an intimidating glare, "you have no reason to be here in this gym other than the fact that you have some great parents who believe in kids having chances in life like they had."

I hear ball bouncing and the guys shooting and missing. I don't hear many balls going in, but I don't look away to confirm. "Your people, they have made the best out of their chances. I believe in chances as a coach, but not for you to play basketball. I believe young men and women should have a chance in life to do their best at whatever it is they choose to do, as long as it is positive."

"Yes, Coach, I hear. And I understand."

"No, don't you give me a standard response, thinking that is what I want to hear. Actions speak louder than words. So far, from what I know about you, your actions spoke in a way. I'm hoping I have not made a mistake to let you come in this gym. As a matter of fact, for giving me that tired line, go run ten laps, and I might talk to you afterwards. Go now, before I change my mind and send you home and maybe let you come back *next* week."

I drop my backpack so fast it might have made a hole in the floor. I start to run with no care about what others think. Dang, I have let my mouth get me in another situation.

I finished the ten laps and run over to Coach Barker. I try to have the demeanor of I'll take whatever he has for me, but not in a challenging way.

"Young man, I made some mistakes that will forever impact my being and my family. I shared with your mother my failures and missteps. I was involved in gang life. I used the excuse of a major knee injury that kept me from finishing my college basketball career, where I was the leading scorer in my conference. The pro scouts were projecting me to be a mid-first-round draft. A shattered dream threw my life out of bounds, when my knee kept me from playing pro."

A ball rolls over and stops at Coach's feet. He reaches down, picks it ball up with his big hand like it was just a baseball, and shoots it one-handed from thirty feet away. It hits nothing but the bottom of the net.

Funny, the gym has been silent since I was sent running, but now, I hear a loud, "Ooh" and "ah" and some "oh, wow" comments.

"Mr. Tingle, my attitude disrespected myself. I let some friends influence me who only wanted me to live life in a downward spiral, like they were. I followed. And I was leading a life I hated. I made justifications through lies and denials. I stepped on snakes in the grass and knew they were biting my life away.' I ignored doing the right thing."

Coach speaks with his huge hands. My eyes can't help but notice them. I find myself transfixed by his hand gestures.

By this time the players who were outside are inside and shooting around, but I know their eyes are on me. It makes me wonder whether everyone knows about me and what happened. But maybe I'm thinking about something that does not matter.

"Mr. Tingle, wait here." Coach walks away and over to a corner, where a few players are hanging out and not doing anything. I watch his long arms and sizable hands point to the door. One of the players walks slowly out of the gym. I believe it is the player who threw the ball at me.

Coach approaches me while speaking at the same time. "I have no time for people who are not going to work hard," he says. "We can all be replaced. I'm about chances, but do not take me for granted. I'd rather lose with players who have a great work ethic rather than win with players who only think about themselves and not the team."

"Coach, may I speak?"

He nods. I want to be real with the coach, and it takes me a little while to get my words to come out. "I knew my friends were doing something wrong. I acted as if it had nothing to do with me. But it did."

"What about your grades? Why should I believe you now know better?"

"Coach Barker, give me a chance to prove to you and to my parents and my teammates that I know my education is the most valuable tool I can have to increase my opportunities.

"A chance is earned. Let's see if you will work hard in every aspect of your life from here on out."

"Coach Barker, I recently saw a tattoo on the arm of an older woman. I thought it strange she would have one. I don't see any on your arms."

The coach holds out his arms. He also has shorts on and no visible tats there, either.

"I don't have any, and I'm no longer a follower. I'm my own man, and tats are not for me. If you going to play basketball here, you will not have any visible tats showing. That young man who left the gym, he chose to be over in the corner, showing off his new tattoo on his neck, instead of working on his game and not distracting others from the goal of team first. The purpose to coming in this gym is to be a leader, a better player, a better man, when all else is said and done."

"Coach if you don't mind me asking, what made you turn around your life and start to think?"

"Sadly, I was in the wrong place at the wrong time and with morally wrong people. I witnessed a tragedy. I will not share with you the details, but there is never a day that it doesn't influence my daily walk. Those were the worst days in my life.

"I was arrested and charged. A lawyer came to visit me who had once played for my college coach. He made statements to the judge and presented evidence that I had done nothing illegal, just was only in the wrong place. The judge was in control of my life, it was up to his discretion. He dropped the charges. My college coach asked me to join his staff as a student coach. He did not give up on me, once life was no longer about me playing basketball. He wanted me to help talk to young men and to help him be a better coach, as times were changing.

"Now I give you a second chance. So, go run twenty-two times around the gym at full stride. Then you can join the open gym scrimmages. Oh, and know the varsity players will come at you hard. They are not your friends or teammates, unless you can hold your own. Be ready to battle, if you want to play on this team."

'I run the twenty-two laps at such a pace, others in the gym say when I run by, "Slow down! You're making us look bad, next time we have to run laps."

I run faster. The gym has been off-limits while I've been on restriction. So, I'm not wasting this opportunity.

It is the third game when Coach Barker puts me on a squad. I need to have confidence in my skills. I am ready for war, much like Toussaint Louverture, based on what I've read on the Internet and watched on YouTube.

I expect to hear smack talk in an attempt to distract my game and take away my confidence. My game is about being one step ahead and having counterattacks ready. My dad has instilled that in me, from when he and I play chess.

Once I'm on the floor with JV players, I can quickly tell some of these players lack skill. They turn the ball over three times in a row to the better of varsity players, who talk smack and play bully ball. They trap or double-team the JV players when they try to dribble the ball up the court.

I make sure I get the ball inbounds the next time. I break through a double team and dribble past the ball defenders with ease. I have skills from all the hard work I've put in, and I challenge myself to play like Stephen Curry, Trae Young, and Ja Morant. My dad talks about Michael Jordan's all-around game and his creative, competitive instincts like no other player he has seen or known, so I've been watching his games and clips on YouTube, too. Plus, I can jump like no others, my friends say.

I keep my dribble and direct one of the guys on my team to move away, so I can't be double-teamed by his man. When he clears out, I move quickly to break to the hoop, leaving my defender behind. I lay the ball up for two points.

I heard the chatter of "*Oooh*" from around the gym.

Then, I'm back on defense, and the varsity player I'm guarding starts talking. "You can't guard me, freshman," he says. "That was a lucky basket you made. Now, I will make you pay for scoring on the varsity."

He dribbles in front of me, trying the same move to the basket I just did. But his crossover is slow and weak. Like Toussaint Louverture, I make chess moves to be ahead of my opponent's move. I poke the ball free and steal it. Then I break hard and go the other way with the ball.

I see the varsity players quickly get back on defense. My defender is right behind me. I pull up to the three-point line and shoot. The ball goes through and touches nothing but the bottom of the net. Then I head back down the court, ready to play defense again.

The varsity players huddle up as they come down the court. Frenchie, the best player on the team and all-league, is six-foot six, a few inches taller than me, and he is staring me down. He comes down the court well under control, looking assured of himself.

"*Switch!*" I yell over to the player guarding him. I can tell he wants me, and I'm not scared.

Now, he dribbles to the top of the key toward my direction. The gym goes into a quiet rumbling of voices as he quickly moves to drive to the basket. I'm ready and slide my feet. I beat him to the spot, and the only thing he can do is shoot or run me over for an offensive foul—a charge. He runs me over, and he puts extra into it and makes me hit the floor hard. I slide on the floor for about six feet.

I slightly feel the wind go out of me, but I'm okay. I pick myself up off the floor and stare at him. Coach Barker loudly calls offensive foul, a charge. I can tell Frenchie is heated to the point he is not paying attention.

The JV team inbounds the ball, and I take it. I dribble fast and do a crossover past the only defender in front of me at half court, leaving him behind me. Then, it is just me and the basket. I dribble past the free-throw line, and I dunk the ball. Dunking is easy for me.

The gym grows loud as players high-five me or dap me up. I have been dunking for over a year, but I only dunk while goofing around with my friends. I stay focused and go back to play defense.

My team loses, but the game is close, and I played very well. After open gym is over, Coach Barker has me run twenty-two more times around the court, and I run them just like before.

When I leave the gym, I notice those varsity players who talked smack earlier are quiet when I walk by. I head to the bus stop feeling good, but I know I need to stay humble. I want to be more than good. I want to be great. My dad says playing is easy when someone practices hard.

As I stand at the bus stop, Frenchie pulls up to the curb in a car. He rolls his window down. "Hey, freshman, my bad on the charge. I wanted to know whether you could play in the heat of battle. It looks like you can play and help the team. I'll see ya' next week, freshman."

"My name is Marley."

"Marley got game. Cool," he says as he pulls away.

Chapter 14

I take a seat in the library, hoping to see the little old librarian. I need to return the paperback version of *The Diary of Anne Frank* and take the book to the checkout counter, returning a history lesson. The librarian who checked the paperback out helps me.

I now want to read more history, but I'd like the little old librarian to guide me. Plus, I kind of think she knows what happened in the room when I traveled back in time and ended up in someone else's body.

I also wonder about my chair vibrating when I was on the deck with Alana. What was that trembling I felt? She didn't seem to feel or see me shaking... but what was that? Should I be living in fear?

I think back on the life and times of Toussaint Louverture. He came through a period in history when a man and woman's life had no value, so he fought for the freeing of enslaved people in Haiti. He had every reason to live in fear. However, he unleashed a country from slavery and helped create a nation.

My sisters, Elvina and Cherri, walk into the library. Mom has asked me to spend some time with them, helping them find books we can read as a group. Mom and Dad have always made clear we are family and a team, responsible for teaching one another. I enjoy reading to my sisters, although they are old enough to read independently and do that, too, of course. But we also read aloud to each other, to make us better readers.

I want to find some books that highlight women warriors, scientists, and politicians as world changers. And although maybe not an accurate word, we often say that a man is a *hero*, but when it's a woman, we use the new term, *shero*. We have studied historical figures in school like Harriet Tubman. We know about some great women athletes, like Venus and Serena Williams, and going back to Althea Gipson. My sisters have watched the WNBA, ever since they began to play basketball.

We are all tall for ages. We get our height from our grandparents, who are over six feet tall. And Mom is taller than Dad. I spend time working with my sisters on their game. My sisters are fans of Candance Parker, A'ja Wilson, and Sue Bird. They love Te'a Cooper and super-love Chinenye "Chiney" Ogwumike from Nigeria, whom they see on sports channels as a commentator. My sisters love how she has sisters who play basketball, and all of them are academic scholars. Elvina wants to study sports broadcasting and be like Maria Taylor.

Present-day sports stars, social media figures, and even less iconic women, like my mom and grandmother, have made it clear that we all need to know about women from all time periods.

My mother has taught me about a woman's worth by example. I want my sisters to know the same thing. I want to be a young man who leads by example, so my sisters know they are unique and should always expect to be respected by men.

We gather some books and then sit in the corner of the library on a rug and oversized pillows. The library has books laid out on a round table, each one with reader postcards that includes a book synopsis and sometimes a comment. You can take the postcards for future reference and to encourage people to read those books.

My sister Elvina had one of those postcards she'd collected earlier, about a book titled *King Peggy*.

The postcard synopsis read:

A Black American woman goes from clerical support in an office and unexpectedly finds herself leading a vastly changed life as a king. King Peggy becomes the leader of a traditional African town with little to no running water or education system for the youth. King Peggy helps uplift and transform her community into a modern functional village. A stranger-than-fiction tale, but the true story of a woman who made a difference in her town and country by leading.

All three of us loved the movie, *Black Panther*. We were so excited when we watched the women's fighting unit in the fictional Kingdom of Wakanda. One of my sisters found an article online from the BBC, the British Broadcasting Company, "The Legend of Benin's Fearless Female Warriors." These female warriors were real, in fact. The Dahomey Amazons were female soldiers of the Kingdom of Dahomey, a West African empire on the coast, between Nigeria and Togo, from 1625 to 1894. They resisted European forces with fearlessness.

While I am at the library with my sisters, I never see the little old lady. Maybe it is her day off.

Chapter 15

I'm in bed that night, feeling great, after I showed Coach Barker and the other high school players I could play. I even had the best player show me some respect in a funny way. When I get up in the morning, I plan to do my chores and then get straight back to the gym.

I'm still not asleep, though, and the last time I looked at the clock, which I've seemed to do every half hour, it was 3 a.m. I have been sleeping lightly and dreaming, but then I keep waking up.

I turn over to look at the ceiling. Oh... Is my door opening? I don't hear anything.

I take a deep breath. I want to scream. I try not to. I can't see a face in the dark, standing back against the wall. I try to keep my eyes from being wide open. I don't want whoever—or whatever—is in my room to see me watching them. The room is not tumbling or shaking... Does this have anything to do with Anne Frank?

"Marley," I hear my Mom call out.

Oh, I can breathe again. The light comes on, and I jump out of bed. I see my dad standing in the corner. I'm taller than he is, but I'm still like a little kid when I see him. He has been gone for two months, and I thought he was not due home for another month.

I hug my dad, and his strong arms embrace me. We don't let go until my mom comes into the room with my sleepy sisters. When they see our dad is home, they are immediately wide awake and screaming at the top of their lungs.

"Hey, quiet down before the neighbors think we are in here cooking all three of you for breakfast, lunch, and dinner in the wee hours of the morning." Mom gives us kids a stern look and also our dad, but then she smiles at us.

"Dad, what are you doing here?" I ask, amazed. "I just talked to you the other day, and you were in Germany."

"Well, all of you quiet down before your mom puts us all out."

We look over at mom, who is crying like a baby. Now, she's the one who is loud, and we all laugh.

"My advanced class accelerated the speed of the course, so the mechanics could get back to their dealerships, and so I could get back to my family."

After all the excitement, my parents head back downstairs, and I go to sleep quickly feeling safe for the first time since I saw Anne Frank's eyes.

When I wake in the morning and go downstairs, my mother has a beautiful, wide smile on her face, something I haven't seen in a while.

I also know my dad will work me out harder than ever before, and I'm excited to prove to him that I'm not afraid of hard work.

⚜

"Honey, you should come with us."

Dad is behind the car's steering wheel, talking to Mom through the rolled-down window. She waves him away with her golden smile.

My dad is taking us to an African American history exhibit. He wants to spend time with the whole family, but Mom wants Dad to spend time with us kids first. My sisters and I are in the car ready. We've really missed our dad.

Before we go to the Seattle historic King Street Station exhibit, we go to breakfast. It is a tradition for Dad to take us to the soul bistro, a small restaurant in the central part of Seattle. Dad tells us about sitting outside and eating breakfast almost every morning in Germany and other neighboring countries he visited. We listen intently as we eat the best French toast and fried chicken.

"While I was in France, I had an opportunity to sit at an open-air bistro and have great conversations with many people from different parts of the world."

"Dad, were you scared while over there?" my sister Elvina asks.

He replies, "We can be frightened by unusual views, sounds, and other peoples whom we don't know and who have a different culture. We can become suspicious and distrustful with the unknown. It is like seeing the people in here, at breakfast. Why should I be scared of them? Look around at each person for a while."

We all look at each person in the restaurant without staring to long.

"Now, tell me, is there anyone in here who frightens you? And if so, why?"

The three of us all shake our heads no.

"The reason you have no fear is you are in familiar surroundings, in your own city. Somehow, we convince ourselves to feel fear when we are out of our normal settings. That is self-inflicted superstition and a fear of things you don't understand."

Then Dad tells us, "Stand up. All three of you, stand up for a second and sit back down."

We do.

"Now, did you think the chair would now not hold you, when you sat on it with your weight? You never thought about it. You had no fear, and you didn't create any doubt in your head.

"Look out the window. We can see cars going by, and some are going over the speed limit. Have you thought for one moment that a car would drive *into* this place? Nope, you have not. But all things are possible. We should try to avoid creating negative scenarios.

"The owner of a bistro I loved to visit was from Egypt. You may learn about how Egypt spans the northeast corner of Africa and is a Mediterranean country. Some of the bordering countries and nearby regions are the Gaza Strip, also known as part of Palestine, and Israel, Sudan, Jordan, Saudi Arabia, Greece, and Turkey.

"Egypt has one of the oldest documented and written histories in the world and is part of the cradle of civilization. Some of the earliest developments in writing, the cultivation of food production, modern sprawling cities, organized religions of Christianity and Islam are attributed to Egypt. We still use sciences from centuries ago, and governmental structures were developed in Egypt.

"The Great Sphinx is there, too, and the majority of its people live near the banks of the Nile River. My friend, the bistro owner, grew up in Cairo and lived in other major cities along the Nile Delta. He was raised in orphanages and moved from one to another until he aged out of the system. He washed dishes, swept floors, and did food prep as he watched the chefs and cooks until he became older.

"Oh, and let me mention, I hope all of you are offering to help your mom in the kitchen. The fellow I speak of, he learned all about foods made in the region, from Mediterranean dishes to Egyptian and many African foods.

"He eventually moved to France and became a well-known chef in restaurants. However, his goal was to own a small little bistro, making fresh bread and serving different coffees and sandwiches. He wanted to feed his community. Wealth was not his driving force."

"Hey, Dad, are we going to feed the homeless again over the Thanksgivings weekend, like we did last year?" Cherri asks.

"I would like to think we always do, even when you become adults on living on your own.

"When I met my friend from Cairo, he was content and happy, serving people in need. He told me the story of Mansa Musa and the Empire of Mali. The Sultan of Mali was the richest man ever. He spread his wealth, built cities and universities, fed the poor, and constructed temples. Mansa Musa made safe trade and transportation routes all through sub-Sahara Africa. I read a lot of Google information and stories about him on my tablet while on my long flight home from Germany. I want each of you to read about ancient Egypt."

My two sisters claim my dad's tablet before I can speak up. I decide to check the library for books about Mansa Musa. After listening to my dad's story, I know I want to read a book about Mansa Musa and those times.

Dad said the Sultan of Mali was living somewhere around 1300 AD.

❧ ❦ ❧

We enjoy the history exhibit and learn some troubling history of the growth of America. However, we also learn how people overcame and became great Americans. Thousands if not millions of people, some who look like me and some who don't look, had good hearts and intentions. Together, they saved, fought, invented created ways, and overcame tough times. They made America full of promise and hope. That promise and hope is still a struggle, to make opportunity possible for all. I read about how some people disapprove of the teaching of the shameful things in the world and aspects of American history.

My dad keeps his word. He said he would work me out harder than I knew I could, and on the following two days, dad has me running twice a day.

I run wind sprints with no rest and run hills and stairs. He has me doing a lot of other physical challenges, too. I sleep so hard each night.

I am worried about the coming Wednesday's open gym. I wonder whether I will have any energy. Dad gives me the next two days off with only a light jog and stretching plus some relaxing swim laps at the pool.

Chapter 16

I walk into the gym sure the coach will not make me run extra laps, after how well I played last week. Wrong. I imagined he would let me play with the varsity players after competing and making some look less skilled than I am. Wrong, again. I have it all wrong from the moment I walk into the gym

"Marley Tingle," coach shouts, "start running twenty-two laps now, and then warm up with the JV players."

I drop my gym bag and start to run. The guys say nothing to me, as if worried they might get in trouble and have to run with me. I run steadily with my gifted legs and make sure the coach and players know that no one can keep up with me.

After my laps, I approach the JV players. They do not greet me or have much to say. I believe I know why. The way I played last week and how I took over when they were getting beat badly, I think some of the players might feel like I am above them. Or some might feel the varsity players will go harder at them now. Maybe they think I will treat them badly, not show them respect. Or maybe that I won't be friendly if I make varsity. If it is any of those reasons, it is a destructive mindset.

Maybe my talent is good enough to make varsity, but we are freshmen, and they will be my classmates. So, they are who I want to be around.

I step toward my future classmates. "Hey, guys, we can run with the varsity." They look at me as if they don't trust me. I can see at least one of them has an attitude toward me. The tallest kid on the squad tries to stare me down.

I continue to talk, hoping to prep up the guys I'll be playing with. "They may be a little stronger and faster. They put the work in, meaning they have been in the gym, shooting, running, and lifting weights."

"Why are you over here acting like you're our coach?"

I was right. The player wearing a Miami Heat jersey with Shaq on the front has an issue with me. He turned the ball over more than anybody last week and was a ball hog before I stepped on the court. I ignore him but someone else doesn't let him tread on the message.

"Let's hear what he has to say," my friend Hakim says. "I want to play, but I don't want to get beat down just to say we were on the court with the varsity." He makes his point clear."

I ignore the player who is on another mental team and not with us. This is a way to improve our skills, by playing against guys with better skills.

"We can compete if we try to out hustle them for every loose ball. Let's fight for every rebound and get back on defense. Do not let them intimidate you with 'in your face' smack or physical contact. Box out and box out hard."

I see a few nodding their head.

"The coach will not let varsity players disrespect us with hard fouls. If you guys run hard, I'll pass to you, and if you are not open, I'll take the ball to the hole or shoot an open shot. Come on, guys, don't back down."

I place my hand in the middle of the group. All the guys add their hands on top, even the Miami Heat player with the bad attitude.

Hakim says, "Team on three."

And on three, we do a loud chant, *"Team!"*

Our warmup is much more spirited. All I said were things I've heard in different forms from my mom and dad and grandparents. When I was teaching my little sisters to ride their bikes without training wheels, they fell off, but I convinced them to try again, and now, of course, they ride with no fear.

I look toward the varsity players, who are studying our energetic approach to warming up.

Frenchie, the six-foot six senior, nods my way. I assume the varsity squad is out to beat us JV players with a lopsided score. I know I must play well and push my teammates.

I think about what my dad told me and my sisters about the bistro owner, his friend who took advantage of every chance while growing up in Egypt. I look at playing with the JV players against the varsity team as a chance to be on varsity.

The game starts. The varsity guys play fast and physical, but we JV players stand tall in our effort. If a varsity player misses a shot, we grab the rebound and chase down all the loose balls. They pass the ball to me, and I help them score.

Frenchie guards me, and, as my friends would say, I give him the business. I out-play him for the first half of the game. I'm quicker than he is, but he is bigger and stronger. He outplays me in the second half of the game, but not by much.

The coach mixes JV and varsity players in the second game. Frenchie and I are on the same team. At the opening tip, I get the ball and do a crossover to fake out a player before throwing a high pass to Frenchie for an alley-oop dunk. He and I and two other JV players and another lower-level varsity player beat the other team, which has four varsity players and one JV player, and we beat them convincingly.

After the open gym, my dad picks me up. I have a better time telling him about talking to my freshman teammates than about my game play at open gym.

"Son, leadership has the greatest potential to lead you to being a great player."

Chapter 17

When Dad drops me off at the library, Alana is there, sitting on the steps. I asked my parents could she spend some time with me at the library, and they said yes. But first, I received another reminder that this is a reward for applying myself to reading books and retaining what the books offer.

Alana stands up at the top of the stairs, and because I'm six-foot two, we are eye to eye, even though I'm still two steps below her.

Because we are blinded by our attention to each other, we block a few people who want to come up the stairs. They are elderly and need the handrail we are leaning on.

"Oh, we are sorry," I say quickly. "Let me get the door for you."

A few more few elderly people get off a bus as a group and walk past Alana and I hold the door.

"Oh, what nice young people, and thank you," we hear from each person.

Alana helps one lady with a book bag who might be trying to carry too many books. We let the group all go in the door, and then we stay outside for a while. The sun is behind the tall trees that surround the library, but they cannot lower the heat from this summer day.

People often sit on blankets on the grass around the library grounds.

"Marley, it is really nice you asked to see me."

Her smile makes my day instantly better, and I was already feeling good after the way I played in the open gym.

"You asked permission for us to meet at one of your favorite places... Or should I say, the only place you can go?" She laughs and covers her mouth trying to retain her laugh.

"Oh, okay, I see you, silly girl. Your turn is coming for me to get you back one day."

"You just make sure we can go to the Pike Place Market, when you are allowed. Don't back out. I still want to go."

"Alana, I wouldn't miss going down to the Market. Look, I don't want to come across as weird or anything, but you know that you're my bestie, right?"

"If that is right, then don't get in any more trouble. We're about to go into ninth grade, high school. So, chill out with the bad grades and other stuff. Now we're at the library, why'd you want me to be here, instead of coming over to your house?"

"If I tell you, maybe you won't believe me." I look around the inside of the library as we walk in. I know the tables, chairs, and books, and walls are real, but I had an unreal event in my life here, between these walls. "I want to show you what I think will happen..."

"What is it? You keep kind of acting strange with questions, and the things you speak about has me tripping out on you. Let's get a seat. And stop acting weird before I go tell your mom to take you to a doctor. You act as if you have fallen on your head."

"Well, I kind of did."

"Stop it. You don't need no help being crazy."

Crazy, huh? Well, look at who is hanging with me, if I'm so crazy."

"Good point. Let me go sit over here, away from you." Alana acts as if she is about to run but nods her head for me to follow her.

Just as we sit down, I see the old librarian pushing the book cart. I grab Alana's hand and lead her over.

The lady has turned the corner around a long bookcase. When we go around the corner, I don't see her.

"Are you looking for me?" I hear from behind me.

I know I must have a look of surprise, wondering how she came up behind me. The sun streams through the tall windows of the library, giving the very short librarian a glowing halo around her white hair.

"Ah…, excuse me, ma'am. I want to let you know I finished *The Diary of Anne Frank,* and I have read other books since I last saw you."

She places books on the shelf. "Keep reading, so you are free in every aspect of your life. Decisions are required of each person to place themselves in circumstances of learning. Knowledge will always be your protector."

"Yes, ma'am, I think I understand. I brought a friend."

"Do you and your friend want to know why I wanted you to read about Anne Frank? If so, please, follow me."

I look toward Alana, who has a blank expression and seems confused. Her eyes are wide and unfocused. We follow the librarian to the elevator.

We enter a narrow hallway, where we wait for an elevator, which is slow coming. Once we are on, it takes a super-long time to reach the bottom floor. After we three exit, the librarian leads us to the room with short, quick steps.

I scan the room where I experienced my life-altering time travel event into someone else's body.

The librarian wears a blouse similar to the day I met her, when I first saw the tattoo near her wrist. Inside the room, she slowly rolls up her sleeve. Alana covers her mouth after exhaling a long, startled breath.

We both can now see the tattooed numbers on the librarian's inner forearm. Alana's reaction tells me she understands what they mean even before I do.

The librarian's eyes connect with mine in a way that completes the story of the day I asked about her tattoo.

This woman before me was once a young person whom the Nazis registered with a tattoo on her arm, categorizing her to work in a concentration camp, where so many others were sent to die. She is a Jewish Holocaust survivor of the extermination camp, Auschwitz. The little old lady repeats her mantra about reading so I will not imprison my mind through lack of knowledge.

We exchange no words as she rolls her sleeve down. I put my hand on her shoulder and think, *What can I say?*

"I survived."

We stand in a long silence until we notice a much older man and woman exit from one of the reading rooms in the basement. The two move slowly with walkers, and I recognize two of the people Alana and I helped enter the library. I think to ask whether I can help again now. But before I do, the old librarian places her hand on my forearm and shakes her head *no*.

I realize I did not ask out loud; I only thought about asking. She must have been able to tell from the look on my face what I was thinking.

"Ma'am, I want to read a book about Mansa Musa, the Sultan of Mali, or any books about that time, from that region in Africa or northern Africa to as far as Egypt. I want to read a book with Alana, my best friend, and I'm sure she wants books you would want her to read."

The lady stares up at me. She has to know... She must know. How could she not know about my time travel?

"Young sir and young lady, I am all too happy to help you on your journey to know this world of the past. What things seem on the surface are only a pinch of salt on what lies underneath our centuries of history." She points to all the old books.

"When I came to this country, I wrote poetry for the literature class I taught, my first job in America. I want to share it with you two, in hopes it will help you to stay in tune with what the world offers you and what you can present to the world to make it a better place..."

We stand on different grounds

Yet we are near the same shores, mountains, and valleys

The rivers that flow from the mountain and out to the sea, we float by each other

The roots of the trees that drink the same waters right alongside us, should we not stand together under them?

If we share the same shade, fruit, and the shelter the trees provide, we share our knowledge of how to have better days?

The knowledge of man has not walked on solid ground

We have repeated the same mistakes all through humanity

Centuries, decades, years, and down to the countdown of all times, we have failed to live in one accord

How do we share our fields?

Streams of love for mankind will nurture our thirst

I am reaching out to you

As bad seasons along the way have taught me valuable lessons

For sure, the grounds under us can be solid and firm

Please do not let me stand alone for a better humankind

She finishes. and I think about each line, wishing I had recorded all she said.

"Wait here in the room. I will return with the books you have requested."

We watch her enter the elevator before Alana says, "Marley, she is a part of history, and we are in her presence."

"I know."

Suddenly, the elevator door opens again. That's weird! How did she come back so fast? She has two books in her hands and places them on the table.

"Here. Please read these two. Much like what you read in *Animal Farm* and in *The Diary of Anne Frank*, the message is, the whole world can be in your hands through books. Young man, and to you, young lady, I have been saying, you must read, or the world will imprison you. I don't mean that in a sense that you will go to a physical prison with bars and guards. It is more about a mindset of closing yourself off from opportunities. Through books and other forms of research, you might be the next— Wait."

A cellphone appears in her hand from somewhere behind her. She holds it up high, to read the screen.

"Nelson Mandla, James Baldwin, Maya Angelou, Arthur Ashe, Ruby Bridges, Sojourner Truth Medgar Evers, Langston Hughes, Crispus Attucks, Benjamin Banneker, Mary McLeod Bethune, Shirley Chisholm, John Henrik Clarke, John Coltrane, Benjamin O. Davis, Jr.,

Frederick Douglass, Duke Ellington, Marcus Garvey, Fannie Lou Hamer, Matthew Henson, Jack Johnson, Elijah McCoy, Oscar Micheaux, Adam Clayton Powell, Jr., Colin Powell, August Wilson, Richard Wright, Alvin Ailey, Dr. Charles Drew, W.E.B. Du Bois, Henrietta Lacks, Malcolm X, August Wilson, Sam Cooke, Haile Selassie–the once Emperor of Ethiopia and Berry Gordy, Prince, Nipsey Hussle, and Stacy Abrams."

Then Alana asks in a high, snappy voice, not her usual slow, soft tone. "You know who Nipsey Hussle is?" This surprises us both.

Another group of elderly people leave another reading room and enter the elevator. The door closes with what appears to be a lot of people on board. I wonder why I have not heard all those people talking or anything. I never knew they were down here in the basement with us.

The librarian replies, "I have survived beyond many who have not. One should always grow, both regarding life in the here and now and in times long before us and about others who are no longer with us. I want to know who brings or who brought change. I have read down a list of names. History is thousands of years of the world evolving from African descent. You need to know this and how it might impact your lives.

"The birth of all people, their DNA, came either through love or immoral conquerors. Yet, all too often, Black, Brown, Asian, Native American, and many more people of color do not appear in books. You should seek knowledge, even if you dig into places some may not want you to examine. I ask of you, please read like it is food to live by, so you do not starve the mind.

The elevator opens and several elderly people exit, more of the people who got out of the bus, and we held the door open for them. They all acknowledge our librarian as if they are friends and then head into rooms with no windows.

"I want to help educate you with historical viewpoints. Then, maybe you'll stop people from doing wrong."

She turns and walks away, but her comments continue to resonate with me long after she leaves the room. I'm in this basement today because of the wrong I let happen. When my friends stole, I turned away from doing the right thing. Also, my poor grades took my life in a different direction than I should ever want.

"Marley, she left her phone," Alana notices, picking up the cell phone.

"Oh, yeah, she did. I'll take it to her. I'll be right back."

I try to catch her before she enters the elevator, but the door has already closed. The woman moves fast.

I run and leap up the stair to catch her. On the main floor, I find the elevator door is open, but she is not anywhere in sight... *Huh?* I look around to the library, but I still don't see her.

I take the phone to the desk. The other librarians are out on the floor, so I reach over the counter and place the phone down low by the computer keyboard. I don't know why, but then I pick the phone back up and look at the screen. It seems to be off. I push the *on* button, and nothing happens. I put the phone down where I don't think anyone will see it. Then I write a note and leave it on the keyboard.

When I come back into the reading room, Alana is excited. "The lady brought us some note pads to take notes," she tells me. "She wants us to research for more history on anything we read."

"Wait, she came back? I didn't pass her while I was upstairs or coming back down. And I didn't see the elevator go up or down, either."

"Well, you had to, silly guy. Anyway, you read this book. I like the one I have." Alana punches me in the arm. I nod to let her know whatever.

"Alana," I say, gathering up the new books, "let's go upstairs and sit out on the reading deck. The weather is nice." I have changed my mind about whether I want to chance Alana time traveling with me, so I leave the basement.

The sun is shining bright. We find a table with a sunshade umbrella. I scan the front and back cover of *The Royal Kingdoms of Ghana, Mali, and Songhay: Life in Medieval Africa*, written in 1995 by Patricia McKissack and Fredrick McKissack.

Starting around 1300 AD, the kingdoms of Ghana, Mali, and nearby regions were rich with gold and salt. The fortunes stretched across Africa. Mansa Musa, the king, was the richest man who ever lived.

After reading it for an hour, I know I like this book. It's taking me on a journey to Africa, where I'm reading about cities, universities, and the trade of treasures.

Alana pulls my book down to look me in the face. "Marley, I'm into my book. I love it. *Zenzele: A Letter for My Daughter*. I think it was written in 1997, kind of old, like my mom. The author's name is J. Nozipo Maraire"

"My book is about a caravan traveling to Mecca at least two hundred years before Europeans sailed across the Atlantic Ocean, thinking they might fall off a flat Earth, or so they thought."

We laugh to the point where we almost fall out of our chairs.

"What is your book about?" I ask her. "Since you stopped me from reading my book."

Alana smiles widely when she describes it to me. "Okay, I was hoping you would ask. It is the story of a mother who sends her daughter letters of life lessons. The daughter is here in America going to school. There are tales of a dangerous Zimbabwe during the struggle for independence.

"Zenzele's father is a protester and lawyer, which was very dangerous. There is a guerrilla night-fighter aunt who teaches school during the day and a cousin who is a spy but cleans rich people's homes in her effort to spy. I love spies. That's why I think my book has to be better than yours. It looks like you might be riding a camel from empire to empire. Might you see yourself as a king?"

"Why are you teasing me about my book? I like the story."

"I know, I should be serious. I know that Malcolm X traveled to Mecca and realized how big the world is, with so many different cultures. Imagine being a king, taking an entourage of 60,000 to Mecca with so much gold that gold becomes almost worthless for years to come."

I laugh at her. "Oh, so you ask me about my book, but I see you have read the back cover already, along with the preface, when I ran the cellphone upstairs."

"Yes, I did skim through," she admits. "You know I read fast. I found it so strange school has not taught us many things. How come I did not know hundreds of ships from Africa set sail and must have landed in South America, a full two centuries before other explorers."

"I know, right? I have seen paintings and pictures of statues of people who look African but who lived in South America long before Europeans set sail."

Our sunshade umbrella begins to twist as the winds start to pick up and gust. When it really starts to rock, I stand up to make sure it's stable and won't blow over. I don't want it to fall on us.

Alana grabs on to help me hold the umbrella pole. The wind blows really hard all of a sudden. *Wow!* It feels like, if we hang on to it, we might fly....

Then, with a crack, the umbrella snaps and envelops our whole bodies, sucking us up. Under the umbrella, we feel prey clamping around by a Venus flytrap plant. Our noses are inches apart and the squeezing keeps getting tighter.

My legs and feet feel entirely captured inside the umbrella. I try to shout, but I can't, and I don't believe Alana can, either. Her face is full of fear, which takes my breath away. Or is that from the force of the umbrella enclosing us?

Our eyes lock. We're both terrified. Don't people see us? Are they trying to get us out? I don't hear anyone....

Then, we see fire and sand. We are surrounded by the smells of animals, and we seem to by lying on rugs in the desert! People mill about wearing tan, orange, and white colors. Their hands and feet are a mixture of bronze-colored skin and very dark skin. Sandal straps lace over everyone's feet. Through a slender opening, face coverings expose the eyes of both men and women.

The Muslim kids who go to my school taught me that head coverings convey respect and dignity, and for the women, they display modesty. It is also a male rite of passage into adulthood.

I wear a full-face veil, just like the other males I see around me. I can feel the blowing sand, and I know that everything I wear helps to protect me from the sun and sand.

With her face fully covered, as all the women's faces, all I can see are Alana's eyes, her pretty eyes, but I know it is her. We are sitting under a canopy of white linen curtains. There are other young people with us. The sunset approaches.

Alana takes my hand and opens it wide. She places a mango in my palm. I think the tension of all that's been happening made my hand ball up into a tight fist.

"Marley, you were asleep."

"Asleep. That is not all that is going on. I think I know what happened."

"Marley, I'm scared. I'm so scared. How could we both have awakened here, I felt as if I was asleep... I think I awakened before you. I didn't know if I should touch you. Marley, *what is going on*?" Alana is screaming, but no one around us reacts. It's as if they didn't hear her.

I take Alana's hand. "*Shhh*. This time shift of our lives to somewhere else happened to me before... I went back in time and travelled to Nazi occupation during Anne Frank's life. Remember when I asked if you believed in time travel? Now you know why....

"When I was reading *The Diary of Anne Frank*, I was sitting in the basement, and I went back in time and spoke to Anne. I wanted to show you what took place for me. I thought it could only happen down in the basement. But once we were in the basement, in that little room, I wanted us to leave, to make sure you stayed safe. I guess I didn't do so well in protecting you."

"Marley, you are my best friend. I know you would not have me put me here, in danger, on purpose. I'd rather be here with you, but now I want to get back to where we came from. I want to go to the Pike Place Market. And maybe not visit the library for a while. Let's be at school or be on your parents' back deck. *Please*, help us get back."

"Alana, we have to help each other stay safe. I have your back, and you have mine. I'm frightened, too. But try to stay calm." I listen for a second. "Do you hear the voices of the people talking? It is not in English, but I understand what they are saying. I don't know how, but I do comprehend. They talk like my friend Hakim."

"Hakim, the boy who says he is a ruler in his country?" she asks.

"Yes. He's on the freshman JV team. He says his name means *ruler*, but I don't know if he is a real ruler."

"Marley, what does all this mean?"

"I think it is the language of the West Africa country where Hakim is from."

"Marley, are we in the time of the book you were reading?"

"Maybe... We were sitting on the library reading deck, and the next thing I know, we were swallowed up in that umbrella." I add, "The mango is a West African fruit."

"How do you know where the fruit came from?"

"I don't know. Maybe I heard it from my mom, because of her Caribbean descent. Many islanders there came from West Africa."

She says, "A woman came by and handed it to me. I didn't want to take it, but I reached for it, anyway. It is all so frightening.

"When I was in the house where Anne Frank hid, I followed orders. I could not resist the man in charge. Except once, when I did not turn Anne in."

I look around us. "As you can see, others are sleeping. I overheard someone say we are ninety days into the trip to Mecca. Someone else said we would have several birthdays before we reached Mecca. We have just entered the wasteland, and it is becoming dangerous. There is talk of robbers and evil men kidnapping pilgrims and much worse.

"They also speak of Roman fortune hunters setting traps in the Sahara, along routes leading toward the Niger River. The Romans approached by way of the Mediterranean Sea and traveled through Tunisia before making their way south to the Sahara. They arrived acting as if they wanted fair trade, but they were spies searching for gold and much more."

Three men enter the canopy. I watch others' arms fold and heads bow. Feet and hands stir. I can see we are not the only two who are scared. All talk ceases amongst the young people on the carpets.

"Please, do not be frightened, my young hearts," says one of the three men in a deep, gravelly voice. "You are our future, so listen to be wise." His voice seems to rise out of the sand, but he speaks softly to us. "We are people of peace, when peace comes to us."

Older women enter the tent and pour water into clay bowls that they hand to each of us. They kneel down and speak to each girl. A woman kneels in front of Alana, touching her with an open hand in what I think is a gesture to lend comfort.

Another of the men speaks. "We give our peaceful ways to the sun and the moon to honor our ancestors. We need you to help protect the caravan, so we leave with the covering of the last full moon almost gone. It will give us enough light to scout under low light. We must look for danger. Bandits want to steal our gold, fruit, and women, your mothers. You may think you are too young, but you move fast and can hide better. So, prepare. Drink water, and eat what we have given you. We cannot take water or extra food. Do not overeat, and when the time comes, we go."

The three men came to each of us, took our hands, and bowed to us before they left our tent. We all begin to talk, fearful.

I hear a few mention wanting to run and hide. Alana and I are not sure what is happening. We sit in silence. Hours later, we go to separate areas to relieve ourselves. Then, the three men tell us it is time to go.

We begin to hike over foothills of sand. After miles, when our legs are very tired, we stop and suck the juice from mangos.

One of the men comes to stand over Alana and me. "You two, come with me."

Even though we want to resist, our bodies stand up, unable to reject his orders. We follow behind him.

After many more miles, the man tells us to look over a ridge and remain there, watching.

"Stay here until I come back," he says. "Before daybreak."

We lie on the sand on top of the rugs we've carried all night. There isn't much light. We wait for the man, hoping he'll come back soon, and peer out over the dunes of sand. Out of fear, we stay silent.

I realize I need to comfort Alana. "Take a nap, and I will look out for as long as I can."

"Marley, let's take turns. Right now, there is no way I can rest. Maybe you go first and sleep."

"Okay, but I'm like you, I'm wide awake. But I'll try for a while." I roll over on my back and look up at the stars. There are so many stars. I close my eyes in the hope of getting some sleep.

"What are you doing here? A girl and boy, what are you doing here?"

My eyes fly open. A man stands over us. He is tall and fair-skinned, clothed all in tan cloth. He is sunburned around his eyes. I don't know how he came upon us so silently.

We can't move.

He speaks Italian, a very much different language from what we heard at the camp, but I understand him. Alana inhales as if sucking in all the sand in the desert. I think she wants to scream, but nothing comes out. Then she gasps and takes in another deep inhalation.

I place my finger to her mouth lightly. I do not want her to scream. My temples feel tight, and my head hurts.

The man leans in over us. "I'll say it one last time. What are you doing here? And who are you with?"

I don't say a word. I try, but nothing comes out. I move to stand in front of Alana and feel her hand grip my arm.

"Well, then, since you're not going to answer me, you are useless to me."

In the man's hand, he holds a sword. He is not waving it and does not threaten us with it yet. He stabs the giant blade into the sand with force. Then, quickly, he swoops down and rolls us up in our rugs. He rips cloth from his clothing and covers our eyes.

As though we are ice cubes in a cooler grabbed up by a giant scooper, he lifts us both and throws us over his shoulder.

"Alana, please believe we will be okay," I whisper, hoping she hears me.

The man feels mighty, more muscular than even my dad, which is almost impossible, I've always felt. He marches through the sand with us over his shoulder, and I am six-foot two! I felt us going up and down dunes.

When he stops walking, I hear a fire crackle.

Someone says, "What is this that you have? Is that dinner?"

I hear other men's voices and loud laughing.

"We'll have to bury them," our carrier says. "'Cause if they came to spy on us, we want to have no signs left of where they might have disappeared."

The men laugh. Another man says, "Dig right there in the hot sand and cook them."

Alana and I are still dangling like low-hanging fruit about to fall. The man starts to spin us around as if we were two years old. I try to reach for Alana and hold her.

Then, we stop spinning.

All goes still.

Calm, warm winds touch my face...

Silence surrounds us...

I feel my body go motionless...

I sense the touch of a hand on my arm...

I lift my head and see green grass...

Alana squeezes my arm. She sits next to me. Somehow, we are both on the grass next to the library, sitting on a blanket with our books. The notebooks given to us by the librarian lie at our feet.

I squeeze Alana's hand. "You okay?"

"Marley, we made it back."

"Yes, we did. We made it back."

Alana starts to cry. My face feels sweat or my tears, too.

Next to the notebooks are two nearly eaten mangos.

Chapter 18

Alana uses her cell phone to call my mom and ask her to pick us up. She tells me her legs ache and she doesn't believe she can walk very far.

In fact, both of our legs feel like rubber, as if we walked miles in 120-degree heat. I did run a lot during open gym basketball, so I'm pretty well-conditioned, but I this afternoon, I am stressed.

"Why are you two so quiet? Any other time, you are chatterboxes who can't stop talking." Mom laughs.

If only she knew about our journey...

"I hope you guys read while at the library," she adds, "and didn't just run your mouths to sleep."

After we drop Alana off at her house, I am happy to go home and lie down. Although I am a little afraid of closing my eyes, not sure what might go down. I thought the reading room in the basement of the library was my controlled take-off point for time travel. I didn't know this kind of time travel experience could start from another place. Or that it could start in one place and end in another.

After dinner, I ask my mom if I can call Alana to check on her. When I do, she says she is doing well after taking a long nap. She does not want to talk about what happened, and I agree.

Over the next few days, we speak on the phone about the books we are reading. I believe she felt fear that afternoon and is still trying to get over our cross-time transport. But, a few days later, we are laughing again and talking nonstop about anything and everything.

Dad gets me up early, at 5:00 a.m., before he goes to work, and we go down to the lake. There, he puts me through an extensive workout. Dad has me run on the soft grass, doing wind sprints, agility drills running backward, and jumping rope. Then he put me through a shadowboxing self-defense workout and shows me how to throw a jab correctly, how to slip a punch, and how to move to a strategic position in hopes of avoiding a fight.

"Son, I don't want you to let someone frustrate you, so they or you lash out and end up in a fight. Never let anger make you feel physical aggression is the answer. Let me clarify, never become violent or enraged and jeopardize yourself or anyone. It would help if you walked through life thinking about a plan for mental defense, whenever you're challenged in ways that could devolve into a fight. You be the cooler head. But I also want you to protect yourself. Now, after I show you a few more moves and teach you how to avoid being hit with fists or feet, you get to walk home. I have to head into work."

"Really, Dad?"

He laughs, and I know he's not joking.

I smile on the walk home. I feel happy I have people who love me and want the best for me.

Chapter 19

Over the weekend, Mom and Dad drive us to the ocean for fun family time. My parents could have made me stay home, because I am still on restriction. I am old enough to take care of myself for a weekend. But they include me in the family trip.

Mom and one of my sisters, my Aunt Cherri, go to crafts fairs and what they call the High Tea at the Sea Festival. My other sister goes with dad and me on a fishing excursion on a boat.

A couple of people on the boat do not feel well. They get seasick from the vessel rocking and going over waves. That's what is called being seasick. My family does well, and we catch our fish limit.

As we are offloading from the boat, my sister and I go over to our dad and say, "Dad, we have extra fish, since we made our quota. Can we give some to the ones on the boat who were too sick to fish?"

"Yes, that is what we must do. To have empathy for those who are less fortunate is caring. It is easy only to think about ourselves, which takes away from all, when we are selfish. You two make me proud."

I can tell the other passengers are disappointed by the outcome of the day's events, so we walk over with our fish.

"Hello," Dad says to them. "My children want to share what they caught."

A lady and an older man extend their hands. We all shake. The woman says, "We are consumed with the kindness from you and your children. A corporation gifted us free passes to come on the boat, to help our food bank. Catching some fish would have been nice, but we didn't do too well, being on the somewhat rocky waters. My father here doesn't speak much, due to an illness. He saves his words, but he is a giver in life, and he is more than happy to meet young givers."

"Life's most persistent and urgent question is, 'What are you doing for others?'" my sister Elvina says. "Those are the words of Martin Luther King, Jr."

"Well, young lady, let me add something from Brother Martin, may he rest in peace," the older man says, finding the words he needs to share. "He also said, 'Every man must decide whether he will walk in the light of creative altruism or in the darkness of destructive selfishness.'"

I am sleepy on the ride home from the ocean, and I daydream. I was tired even before we went on the fishing trip. We set out just as the sun rose and we ventured back to shore as the sun was setting near the horizon.

I marched with Martin Luther King, Jr. in my dream. He and I sat in jail, but then I woke up and knew I was only dreaming. My grandmother told me one, "In some ways, dreams are the past, present, or future."

Everyone in our SUV is relaxed, lost in a world of their own. My sisters lie against each other, asleep. My mom has headphones on, and I know she is listening to an audiobook, and Dad is listening to his favorite music artist, Chaka Khan.

Suddenly, I feel a hard trembling. It is the same thing I felt on the deck with Alana, when she didn't feel it. But I know what I felt. And I know what I'm feeling now.

Chapter 20

Tuesday night, I ask my dad if he can take it easy on me in the morning and not run me so hard. I want to go to open gym with fresh legs. We worked hard on Monday, and he took me swimming that morning.

He laughs. "You do remember you are grounded and on punishment?

"Yes, I do."

"Marley, me working you hard is a requirement to show you understand the consequences of your actions, in part. You do understand, right?"

"Yes, Dad, I do."

"We will still work on more self-defense before I go to work," he says, "but I let you off from running. You get the day off, but on Thursday, *hmm...* You better get a good night's sleep."

Dad laughs. I smile. I am thankful, but I take a big breath, thinking about Thursday's workout.

Mom gives me a ride to school for the open gym. On the way, we have a long talk about the Pike Place adventure for Alana and me. She is considering making me take my sisters along.

I do not say anything about not wanting to take them. I figure I'll have to let my sisters tag along, if I do. I love my sisters, but I don't want to have them around all day on that day.

Once I arrive at the gym, like every week since I was first allowed to come and shoot hoops, I have to run laps before playing any games. When I finish running, I jog over to the freshmen and JV players, anticipating I will be playing with them again today.

I notice my basketball archenemy Jamelle is in the gym. This catches me off guard. Why is he here? Jamelle doesn't go to our school. He is a junior playing at a crosstown rival high school. But he is warming up with the varsity players on the other side of the gym. Normally, opposing school players don't scrimmage at another school, when it comes to open gym.

I run into him near half-court. Or, really, he runs into me, and it is on purpose.

"Hey, what's up, dude?" he says with his usual smug attitude.

This makes me shake my head.

"What's up with you?" I ask.

"I'm going to your school. I transferred here. And I'm keeping you on the bench, if you thought you'd get some playing time."

"Ah, Jamelle, I guess you forgot that I dominated you, the last time we balled at the park. You might want to look at the playing time differently, because I work my tail off, so we might be playing alongside each other. That probably is a better assessment of what'll take place."

"There you go, trying to talk as if you might be smarter than me. But no matter. My game is better than yours, *fresssshmon*."

I tilt my head and walk backward away from him. I don't need his drama.

The varsity is on one side of the gym and our freshman /JV guys are on the other side, warming up. We do passing and layups and some work on skills drills. I assume leadership and start to lead dribbling drills. Jamelle and I and a few other players end up at center court, dribbling the ball in front of one another in a dribble-off contest.

There are six players, a mix of both varsity and JV players, to start. Quickly, two of the JV players lose their dribble along with one varsity player; their ball rolls away, and they are out. Now, it is me against two varsity players still dribbling. Another varsity player is out, and the gym grows louder with chatter. Jamelle and I keep our eyes on each other, not on the balls we dribble. Minutes pass, and Jamelle and I are still dribbling. He has skills, but so do I.

He starts talking to me, attempting to distract me. I just smile and stare at him with laser focus while I keep dribbling between my legs and showing off other dribbling drills at high speed. I watch him try to keep up.

All the players gather around us in a wide circle. I start to dribble around Jamelle, doing figure eights and crossovers and dribbling between my legs at high speed. I ask one of the players to pass me a ball while I'm still dribbling, and in the next moment, I'm dribbling two balls, like I am a Harlem Globetrotter doing figure eights around my legs. And I'm going fast. Jamelle tries to do the same. But then, he dribbles the ball off his foot, and the ball rolls away while I am still going.

Being on restriction has given me a lot of free time this summer to dribble for hours in my backyard, which has increased my skills, and they were really good before this happened.

Around the gym, kids make loud *oohs* and *ahs* before Coach Barker blows the whistle and divides us into teams.

Jamelle is on the varsity team. Initially, he and I do not guard each other. Jamelle dominates the freshmen player, Hakim, my African Muslim friend. He's not strong enough. In time, he will be, but not right now. The juniors guarding me, I score over him several times. Then, I steal the ball and pass it to my teammates for a fast-break layup.

Interestingly, the six-foot six senior, Frenchie, is sitting next to the coach, watching. I think the coach maybe wanted to watch Jamelle and how he would play with the other players. With Jamelle on their team, the varsity wins by two points.

We take a water break, and then the next game starts. This time, Jamelle and I guard each other, and Frenchie still did not play.

Jamelle scores the first basket over me. He has a nice jumper. I realize I was close to blocking his shot, so I know now I need to position myself better, to disrupt his timing.

I get an easy layup when he goes in for a steal. Then, Jamelle goes up for his jumper in the next play, and I block the shot. I quickly dibble away and pass to a teammate for an easy score.

Jamelle scores another basket over me, before I come down and hit a deep three. Then, I steal the ball from another person and get a layup.

Next, Jamelle has the ball and is coming down the court. I guard him, guiding him toward the sideline. I make a quick move and knock the ball off of him extremely hard. The ball goes out of bounds off of him. Now we have the ball, and I act as if I'm coming to get the ball, but I back cut behind Jamelle. Hakim passes the ball over the rim, and I go up for an alley-oop dunk. The JV players slap me as we all hustle back on defense.

In the next play, Jamelle has the ball and is coming down the court fast. He purposely knocks me down on my behind. It is a hard foul on his part, and I can tell he doesn't care. He just stands over me, daring me to get up. I get up! We are nose to nose, and he calls me a despicable name that I will never repeat.

"Whatever," I say back to him. "I scored over you, I dunked on you, I blocked your shot. I outdid you in the dribble off. Oh, and for the first time since I've been here, the JV is ahead, with one more point to win.

He shoves me. I'm ready to fight, but I think about what my dad said: "Self-defense is not always about throwing a punch."

"Jamelle, you offensively charged me, and if you didn't know, that is a foul, and it might park you on the bench. You shoving me is that the best you got? We might be on the same team, winning, if you can keep your head in the game and stop fronting, 'I'm so bad.' You have a nice jumper, I'll give you that, but obviously, your game has holes. So, you come at me instead of working at your game. You're being weak."

He throws a hard punch my way. I see the punch coming, and I securely side-step, as my dad showed me. I quickly move to the side, and I'm almost behind him and then shove him away.

There is laughter around the gym. Someone shouts, "Oh, Bruce Lee is in the house!" More laughter comes, but louder this time. I didn't mean to embarrass him, but he lost his cool.

Coach Barker blows the whistle at full volume and calls us over. We have our eyes on each other as we walk to the coach.

"Guys, I'm not going to have this here at this school. Either we learn to play together, or one of you won't be here at all. Jamelle, Marley is enrolled in this school, so I'm gonna say, if you can't get along with everybody, I will not let you transfer here to play basketball. So, fix yourself before you wreck yourself."

Jamelle turns hard and storms out of the gym.

"Okay, you had a choice," Coach says in a loud voice to the back of Jamelle's head as he leaves the gym. "Life is about choices."

"Coach?" I say. "Coach Barker, let me go talk to him. We've been aggressive competitors on the outdoor courts, and he's always been a bit of a hard head, but he could help the team. You gave me a chance. Please, give him a chance. Can I at least try to get him to calm down?"

Coach nods.

I run out of the gym and catch up to Jamelle. "Hey, man, is this what we are doing? You're beefing with me because we go hard against each other? You transfer here, and you want to start a war with me? We could be on the floor together with Frenchie, and you know he has game. It is about us winning. I'm a freshman, and you're a junior. I'll be walking in your footsteps. Let's go hard at each other in practice, to make each other better for the team. We could have a good team.

"Dude," I continue, "come back in the gym. It may be hard to humble yourself, but do the right thing and apologize to Coach Barker. If he makes you run extra, do it."

Jamelle gazes past my head, and I think it may be hard for him to look me in the eyes right now.

He nods, though, and walks past me, heading back to the gym. He and Coach Barker have a short conversation. Then, Coach puts Frenchie, me, and Jamelle on the same team.

We play good defense. We play as a team. The varsity wins the next game 15 to 3 with fast breaks, dunks, three-pointers, steals, and everybody passing to the open man.

Afterward, Frenchie, Jamelle, and I walk out of the gym together. Jamelle nods and walks away, saying to me with a half-smile, "Next week, I'll beat you down in a dribble-off."

"There's not enough hours in a year for you to practice that much," I reply.

All three of us chuckle.

Next, as I catch the bus to the library, I reflect on the life lessons I have learned throughout the summer. One of the most important messages is I must be a leader.

The bus seats are full, so I have to stand, along with a few other passengers. I hold onto the standing passenger pole to secure myself.

Suddenly, I feel that hard trembling again. No one else is reacting, though. It's as if they don't feel what I feel.

Chapter 21

I need to check in both books that Alana and I were reading. She couldn't make it to the library today, so she dropped off her book at my house, for me to return it for her.

I look around for the old librarian as soon as I come in the door. I walk around the stacks and tables, but I didn't see her. I pick up a comic book, something I haven't read in a while, because I've been reading books.

An hour later, I see her pushing a cart. I move fast to reach her, as I want her recommendation on more historical books. A part of me— wants to time travel. I know it is scary, and maybe having Alana with me last time put her in danger. I know I'm responsible for whatever happens, if I take someone along with me. I need to be cautious. Also, I hope to find out what is going on with me, when I have these reoccurring tremors...

"Ma'am, before I fell off from reading on my own, I read a book last year about Black Native Americans in history. I believe it is titled *Black Indians: A Hidden Heritage*. It was in our school library. I think the author's last name is Katz."

"Did you enjoy reading Mr. Katz's book about runaway slaves who often made their way to Native American areas?"

"I did. It seems like it is a hidden history about Black men and women who often found a better life, after the horrors of slavery."

"Excuse me," the librarian says. "I'm a bit chilled. I need to put my sweater on."

I spot a sweater draped over the end of the cart. She allows me to help her put it on. Out through the windows, the tree branches are in the wind. I'm wearing a thicker sweat top, since the weather has changed.

"Now, as we were discussing," she says, looking directly at me in a way that always commands me to listen. "Often, runaway slaves found refuge from slave hunters when they stayed near or with Native Americans. Those formerly enslaved people intermarried with Native Americans, which allowed the creation of a family unit after slavery had stolen away that experience from them."

"Wow, you know so much about a lot of cultures."

"I read to learn about others rather than about myself. Knowledge is infinite. Knowing about many people's cultures—their beginnings, movements by choice or displacements, plights, and victories—is a great reward."

She starts pushing her cart of books and stops to place them on their shelves as she continues to talk to me. "If I encounter someone of another culture, race, or religion, I do not want to be ignorant of their history."

A toddler who has not been walking for very long tries to move fast in front of us. The child stops in front of the librarian and squats down in the aisle, as they do at a toddler's age. The child's face reflects what I've been thinking: puzzlement.

A woman, whom I assume is the mother, comes over and picks up the child, apologizing for her child being in the way.

"Your baby sees what most others don't see." The librarian says and smile at the baby as she talks to me.

"Young man, I don't want to insult anyone because I have no respect or basic understanding of another race, culture, religion, or lifestyle. There are misrepresentations about the children of Native Americans and runaway slaves." She pauses as a thought occurs to her. "Wait a moment. I have some information I printed out on this topic. You should read it. Let me go get that copy for you."

A moment later, she hands me stapled pages that are covered in black-and-white lifelike drawings and a lot of written information.

"Semi-related to the subject you speak of, do you see those pictures up on the wall over there? The third one is Thomas Jefferson, President of the United States. Thomas Jefferson was an enslaver who worked to establish a new nation founded upon principles of freedom. Oddly, Jefferson owned over 600 slave people during his lifetime, the most of any U.S. president. Take a good look at a man to whom many Black people are related. I'll let you figure out how.

"Jefferson hired two men, around the early 1800s, to explore the nearly obtained West. When you walk home or ride in a vehicle or fly over the Northwest, you may be in an area where those men, Lewis and Clarke, may have sat down, laid down, or picked berries.

"Look at all the oak wood in this library. It is from trees that grew before the time of Lewis and Clarke. Please read, and I'll be back later."

I take a seat where I usually sit to read comics, though I have not done that in a while.

"Hey, Marley," says Devon, as he walks over to me.

Devon who I have not seen since early summer is talking too loud in the library, especially when calling my name. I miss hanging out with my friends, I do. But I've had a break from them, and in the future, maybe we won't be best of friends, but just friends. As always, he is dressed like me. His locs have grown a lot, but mine are still longer.

"Yo, man, please don't. I'm being funny. But for real, how has your summer been?"

"My life is good. I'm making the best out of whatever is front of me," I say. "What about you?"

"My mom did not let me off as easy as thought after getting caught shoplifting," he tells me. "She found me a job working on a landscaping crew. It is backbreaking work, and on hot days, it is really tough. My boss don't play. He doesn't even let us wear earbuds to listen to music while working. Look, my hands have cuts and bruises I get every day."

Devon's hands are jacked up.

"Well, you're making money, right?"

"Yeah, I make good money, and I'm saving it. My mother also has me in an evening class about money management. It's a class where I learn about investing, savings, credit, and credit cards and taxes. It is all the things I'm going to need, if I want to own a house and buy a car and be able to get low-interest loans, if I want to start my own business one day."

I hold my finger up to mouth and shush him. "Man, lower your voice."

"Yeah, my bad. You know, I talk loud even in my sleep. Most of the people in the class have already made financial mistakes, and they are trying to recover. This class should help me avoid mistakes when it comes to my future money and how I spend my money. I'm thankful, in a sense, that I got in trouble, but I don't wanna get in that kind of trouble no more. I— I— I think I said I was sorry before, man, but hey, let me say it again. I'm sorry."

"We're good," I tell him. "You stay out of trouble and so will I. What is Carlos up to?"

"Something good and not so good. He has a summer job. Carlos's mom and dad have been separated for quite some time and they weren't on the same page about what was going on with Carlos. He used to play then off against each other to get away with stuff. But with him getting caught shoplifting and with his poor grades, his mom and dad are now friends when it comes to Carlos. They be all over him, double teaming him even if he was to breathe wrong. He's living with his dad now and majorly, check this out, his dad works at the zoo, so Carlos has a job cleaning the poop out of the cages."

We both make faces of disgust and hold them for a long time.

"Devon, you might understand what this means, but at least Carlos is still on the right side of the glass, when he goes home at the end of the day."

"Yeah, okay. Whatever that means, it must be a good thing, I hope."

"It is. But hey, I need to read this." I hold up the stapled pages the librarian brought to me.

"Yeah, and I need to get a book about world economics, where I can get some information on each country, what their currency is called, and how much it is worth. I found some information on Google, but it's not really in depth, and I need to write a report."

I stand, and we give each other a brotherly hug. Then I start reading:

The exploration of the Louisiana Purchase of territories set forth to find useful passages across the western half of the United States, in order to stake claims before the Europeans. Lewis and

Clarke set about to study plants and animals and to map mountain ranges and the plains and forests.

They were to collect information about Native American tribes. Sadly, a Native woman and a Black man helped map the Northwest regions of our country and establish friendships with the local Native Americans there, but are minimized in the true story of the exploration of the Pacific Northwest.

The Black man, whose name was York, was an enslaved person. Lewis and Clark treated York poorly in the worst ways, even though he was a very good naturopathic medicine man, who used what nature offered for healing and prevention. He hunted and did heavy labor, such as pulling boats upstream, digging, and climbing. Clark was his enslaver and told York he would receive his freedom, but his release never came. York saved the life of Clark more than once and helped to defuse confrontations with Native Americans.

The Native woman, Sacagawea, a Shoshone Indian, was relegated to doing dirty work and was also mistreated. She happened to be pregnant while on the journey and forced to keep up, which she did, before and after she gave birth. Sacagawea did translations and other undertakings to help Lewis and Clark.

Those two men have received significant recognition, but there is an untold story of the two people of color who helped shape the early days of trade along the way to the uncharted Northwest. They came right up to where we stand right now. The mapping of lands hurt the Native Americans, who are often called First Nations people in Canada and at the North American borders.

When I finish reading, I feel a sadness for those heroes who never got their due. When I look up, the lady librarian is standing a few feet away.

"Ma'am, thank you for sharing." I feel hesitant to ask a burning question about whether she and I have a shared knowledge. I know she knows how I have time-traveled twice and about how I have had strange trembling feelings afterward. It is time I ask her about it.

"I have a question, if I may ask."

"Ask of books and nothing else, as of right now." Her expression is impossible to read one way or another. I assume she already knows what I want to ask, though.

"Okay," I say. "I have an interest in Black cowboys. My grandfather loves Westerns, and he says they don't show many Black cowboys. He and I watch episodes of the old Western movies, and when a Black man is featured, we tune in more intently. My grandfather speaks about the greatest entertainer, in his opinion—Sammy Davis Jr, who starred in several Westerns. Yet, other than him, we've only seen a handful of other Black actors in Westerns.

"I want to read about Black cowboys who helped settle the West, and I understand there were a lot of them. My grandfather mentioned that the Black cowboys did everything the others did, but they had trouble buying land or keeping it, because of particular laws that prevented Black people from owning land.

"My grandfather and dad took me to a Black cowboy rodeo once, and it was one of the best days I've had. It was nice to see people who looked like me riding horses and do all the different tricks and jobs I've seen on television."

The librarian walks away and beckons me to follow her. She ushers me over to a section of books and hands me *Black Cowboys of the Old West: True, Sensational, and Little-Known Stories from History* by Tricia Martineau Wagner.

Then she walks away. I watch her, still thinking I want to ask her about time travel, but I let her disappear around the corner.

No! I have to ask her, even though she said only to ask about books. I walk fast, but I do not run—I *am* still in the library. But when I turn the corner, I do not see her anywhere.

Maybe she knows what I want to ask and moved somewhere I cannot see her. Or, possibly, she went to the restroom.

I decide to check the book out and head home.

Chapter 22

Mom has one day a week when she has everyone fend for themselves for dinner. Each of us figures out whatever we want to eat. Tonight is it. I warm up some leftovers and then have some apple pie with butter pecan ice cream.

It is a warm early evening, kind of hot. I feel a little worn down from basketball and my walk home from the library. I think about taking a nap, but I'm a little afraid about what might happen if I fall asleep. I'm not sure where that emotion is coming from, though, as sleeping at night is not a problem for me, despite my recent time travels. I decide I just have to accept unscheduled adventures back through history... Still, I have some fear of falling asleep.

I go out on the back deck to relax and eat leftovers for dinner. I start to read my new book about Black cowboys, knowing I might have a time travel journey while sitting on the back deck.

The book paints a picture of the Black cowboy in the 1800s and 1900s. The sun is starting to creep behind the mountains as I find myself deep into the book's tales of turbulent times, when men rode horses as a job in order to forge a path to newfound freedom.

There was no thought or drive to go back to Africa after slavery. After the Civil War, these men and some women were generations removed from knowing anything about Africa. It was now time to create a new world, in a sense. In that unique sense, these were new Americans, even though they were still not fully recognized as citizens wherever they went.

Black cowboys had to have the roughest souls and forceful behavior to ward off aggression from others. This came from those in power who did not look like them or share their background, and who controlled the dominant culture with its anti-Black laws. Some began to join rodeos. They learned lassoing and bull riding, gun tricks and great skills at taking quick aim. These experiences sometimes led to their moving out West and becoming desperados or robbers of cattle, horses, banks, trains, and stagecoaches.

More often, though, Black cowboys were honest and hardworking men. Black cowboys were one-fourth of the wranglers and rodeo riders, cattle drivers, scouts, and wagon train escorts. That is a lot, considering the movies come up well short of saying or showing this fact.

Black men left the South to strive for a different life, one filled with exciting possibilities. They heard stories of open plains, rivers, and streams where they could homestead and earn a living. Some enslaved people who worked on ranching-type plantations had ridden horseback already. Some formerly enslaved people had built the log cabins they lived in, while being slaves. With all these many different skills, these men went out West.

Black cowboys were brave men who faced wooly buffalos, coyotes, bears, stampeding cattle, friendly and unfriendly Native America Indians, and racism and bigotry in the form of made-up on-the-spot laws.

The Black cowboy made money and bought land, when possible, for their cattle to graze before taking them to market on long cattle drives.

✦

I put the book down and decide to watch TV with my family. We watch an old movie about a Black race car driver. It is called *Greased Lightning* and tells the true story of Wendell Scott, America's first African American NASCAR driver. It is both funny and serious.

As my family gets ready to play a board game, I head to bed. I'm super-tired, and Dad will work me hard in the morning. He gave me a day off for basketball open gym, but I know he won't take it easy on me in the morning.

I like the challenge, but I don't let him know that. I would not want him to make it any harder. I'm laughing inside, but not a lot. I need to be ready.

Chapter 23

Wow, it's 4:00 a.m., and already, I hear my dad calling my name. I know he's an early riser, but *this* is the earliest!

"Bring your backpack," he calls up to me.

That means I need to bring water and food. I'll probably be catching the bus home from wherever he's taking me to work out. I am glad he moves my training to different places.

We drive to Alki Beach on the west side of Seattle. It's a long sandy beach that goes on for miles along a waterfront and where you can see all of downtown Seattle across the water. Ferries are visible, too. People ride them both as walk-on passengers and with their cars. I remember how Alana and I caught a ferry after leaving the Pike Place Market and rode back home near sunset.

I look to the sky over the water and can tell the hot weather is coming back

Dad pulls into a parking spot along the beach. "You're running long wind sprints in the sand today."

"Huh? What?"

"Neither of those words constitutes a response that I would like to hear from you. You have to run close to the same interval time each time and then jog back."

I look over the water to calm myself, knowing this will be tough. Dad and I jog for a mile, and then we stretch. He marks off about 100 yards, but he calls it 100 meters, because my dad measures many things by the metric system after working on Mercedes Benz cars and a few other high-end foreign cars, whose nut and bolts and tools are metric in sizes.

I start to run wind sprints as he times me. Something in me pushes me to the point that I want to go faster each time without worrying how many laps I have to run. I want no excuse coming from me about my conditioning, once I step on the high school basketball court. I want to show my dad I can meet his challenge, knowing it will make me better in all I do.

By 6:00 a.m., sweat is pouring off of me like heavy rain. The early morning sun is starting to rise over Seattle. Maybe I'll be lucky and see a whale coming out of the water. It happens often, but not today. All I see is my feet sinking into the sand right now. It is like running in heavy, weighted boots.

"Son, you put in some good work," Dad says when we finish. "I'm proud of you. You didn't back down. This workout will make you a tougher athlete. You won't fear any physical or mental complexities. You will not have anxieties. Instead, you'll take on contests believing in the hard work you put in. That will get you through.

"An old saying I stand by is this—work hard in preparation to generate less stress under competition. I don't want you to fear anything or anyone. Do you understand?"

"Dad, I do. I understand."

On the ride to the workout this morning, I told my dad about what happened at the basketball open gym.

"Marley, you did good. But maybe try talking a little less smack. Showing up a hothead can go wrong. It might help you avoid those situations where someone wants to fight you. Still, I'm proud that you did not get into a fight. You stepped up. Okay, catch the bus home. I'm off to work."

I have my bus pass, my water, and some peanut butter already spread on crackers in a baggie. Also, my headphones to listen to music. My parents monitor my phone calls, because I'm still on restriction, but they have given me back my cell phone for emergency use when away from home.

I walk to the bus stop and wait with the other people who are on their way to work. When the bus arrives, it is full, with only a few seats left to sit. I head to the back of the bus.

I put on my headphones, but I don't turn on any music. I use headphones to block the noise. I pull out my book and munch on my peanut butter crackers from my baggie. I read a little more about Black cowboys. But I'm sleepy, and I find myself staring out the window on the long ride home. The sun is coming up and is bright, almost blinding.

I daydream in the reflection from the bus window about a Black cowboy on his horse, galloping through the fields...

Dang, this bus is bumpy. Wow! We must be hitting every pothole in the city. The padding on these bus seats... Well, there is really no padding. They are hard plastic and tough on my rear end, which is already sore from running. I'm tired and want to get home and go back to bed.

With the last rut we hit, I slightly bump my head on the window, and then I straighten up. The bus begins to hit every single hole, it seems, on the whole West coast. They really need to fix these streets. It seems like it might be dangerous...

Oh no! The bus is flipping and rolling over...! We are free-falling off a bridge... No, *no, no!* I see the water below...

I pull my face out of shallow water. I walk out of a cool-running stream, and my clothes are soaked. I'm barefoot, and the rocks under my feet make me stumble. I struggle to find my balance. I see other men walking out of the stream, too, and they also all have clothes on but are barefoot.

"Hey, that might be the last bath of water we'll get for a long while," a man says to me from atop an all-black horse. "From here on out, it might be just a bath full of dust. But the good news, soaking all your clothes will help keep you cool for a while."

I sit down on the ground and look up at a tall Black man who looks like Coach Barker. I slide my feet into some woolen sox that are full of plenty of holes. I watch the other men, and then I pull on boots as they do. The man who spoke to me trots away.

Unlike my other time travels, I can move freely, but I know I need to do the same as all the others are doing. I pet and stroke a horse that seems to be waiting for me.

Other men mount horses, and I do the same. My butt aches with each step the horse takes. Moments ago, I was on a bus, and I felt each pothole the bus hit. I was already sore from running all those wind sprints, and my thighs and hips were aching. I have a harsh feeling down to my tail end as I and, I guess, *my horse* stroll alongside cattle, who are watering downstream of where all the men soaked themselves upstream.

I see other Black cowboys spaced out, all surrounding a massive herd of cattle. We each wear cowboy hats and ride different colored horses. My horse is brown with tan spots.

A man comes up alongside me. He looks like my... my...my grandfather!

"Hey, Granddad," I say. "What are you doing? Why and how are you here?"

"Who are you talking to? I'm surely *not* anybody's grandfather yet."

"Oh, never mind, sir."

"Young man, drink some water. You do not have time to be out here hallucinating or seeing things. You need to be alert. Let's get these cattle moving again toward that canyon over there."

"Yes, sir."

He gallops away, and I help herd the cattle to head toward a narrowing between the rocky hills ahead. I seem to know what I am doing.

The sun is coming up and it is bright, almost blinding. I reach down for a water canteen, and I take a swig. I need to be careful not to drink too much, especially if we run low. *How do I know that?* I reach into a saddlebag, pull out beef jerky, and munch a large piece.

As I ride my horse, it is jiggling my insides. It feels like I've been riding this horse for weeks as we head into a narrow canyon. I study the rocky hillside and hope rocks don't tumble down. It appears we have thousands of cattle to funnel through the canyon, which will take a long time to move them all forward.

I realize I am on another time travel, but it feels different. I am a part of American history as a Black cowboy, and I seem to be part of something less dangerous than the other times. Before we entered this canyon, I could see a wagon that is being pulled by horses at the very back of the herd. I assume that is the cook wagon.

When we come to a widening of the canyon, I can see tall grass extending far ahead, like an ocean toward a never-ending horizon.

I did not see at first, but there are at least forty Native Americans on horses. They have moved in position in front of us. They all have rifles, and a few have sidearm pistols, too. None of them look like the TV images, with massive, feathered headdresses or other stereotypical details from the cowboys and Indians movies. Most have a feather or two, and most wear long hair braided or bound with leather ties. A few have bow and arrows attached to their backs. There are a lot of weapons, but at the moment, they are all pointed away from our group.

The Native Americans on horseback are blocking the canyon's exit. Each one has positioned their horse about ten feet apart from the next, so they cover quite a distance. A few of our cattle slip through the line, but most of our herd stops behind us, as if the cattle sense trouble.

A man comes galloping up behind me. Once he pulls up beside me, I see he looks like my father. I know it's not my dad, just as I didn't see my grandfather earlier.

The man who resembles my father gets off his horse, and so do I, as does the other man who has been leading or organizing us.

He tells all the cowboys to dismount, as well. Several of the Native Americans get off their horses. A Native man speaks to us in his tongue. The man who looks like my father and the man who looks like my grandfather seem puzzled. I can tell neither of them understand this language. But I know the dialect.

"I understand," I say to them both.

"That is why we brought you along, because you speak Indian languages. So, what is being said?"

I explain, "The great Cheyenne chief, Black Kettle, wants us to turn back. We are approaching their land. He says that agreements with the U.S. government bring broken treaties and promises, and that they have displaced his people. He sees our skin, and he has no fight with us. He knows our people lived as enslaved people. But he can't let any other men take their land as they please."

The man who looks like my father places his hand on my shoulder. "Tell them we're looking for safe passage, and we mean no harm. We don't want land or anything they own. Let him know we share the same brown skin, only ours is just darker. We, too, have been misled by the promise that each man here should have forty acres and a mule. We, too, know about broken dreams and the need to support our families and give them wealth to share and hand down to our children. In 1865, during the American Civil War, the U.S. government agreed upon plots of land for formerly enslaved people, but the government rescinded the order.

"We humbly ask you to let our cattle graze, to keep their weight up. We can only move our cattle slowly, between the rising sun and when the sun hides behind the mountains, about fifteen miles a day. Otherwise, our livestock starts to lose weight. If you help us, we will be able to feed our families and gain some wealth to buy legal lands, which will provide a multitude of means, and we can settle down there and raise our families.

"We will watch our cattle day and night while we pass through Native land, to prevent stampedes. Tell them we are willing to give them ten of their choice from our herd, if they give us safe passage. We have moved to this point over the last month, and we have yet another month to deliver our livestock."

I convey the message to the Native American Indians. The chief discusses it with his men, using hand signals mixed with words in their language. Some are willing and some are not so willing to let us pass through.

The chief holds up his hand to stop the heated deliberation and tells them of another request he will ask of us Black cowboys, and they all seem to agree.

He tells me they want twenty heads of cattle, bullets for their weapons, and dried beef—what I know as beef jerky. The chief knows we have enough to spare. If we agree, we will be allowed to pass through.

I face the men who look like my father and the man who looks like my grandfather and say, "Chief Black Kettle is not requesting but demanding. Otherwise, we will be turning around the herd and losing a month's worth of travel time. He knows we cannot afford to lose any more time. Let's give them what they ask.

"They want twenty head of cattle, bullets for their weapons, and dried beef. They have families to feed and need to protect themselves when other people attempt to come through their land. Chief Black Kettle also said he will give us reoccurring passage, if we trade in honesty."

The men who look like my relatives say okay. I convey the message to the Native Americans. The chief beckons for me to come to him. When I stand in front of him, he hands me a feather from his hair.

"This, my dark-skin young man, is a promise to allow you to pass through these lands."

Then, both parties mount up. As the Native Americans turn and gallop away, I hear a thundering like a storm is passing through the area. But it is not the skies crying out. It is our herd stampeding into the narrow canyon.

The men who look like my father, grandfather, and Coach Barker mount their horses, and so do I. We gallop away as fast as possible.

Suddenly, I am galloping way too fast to stay stable on my horse. I begin to slip and then I'm falling under my horse. My horse's belly is hitting me, and I can't hold on.

Then, my head hits the hard ground...

I'm holding my head. It hurts.

"Hey, are you okay?" An older woman with white hair in the seat in front of me is speaking to me. "You banged your head really hard when we hit that last pothole."

I nod to her and keep rubbing my head. I'm back on the bus, and I have spilled my water. I'm soaked.

But I know my water bottle does not hold that much water...

Everything in my backpack is falling out. On the seat was my baggie that had my peanut butter and crackers A few pieces of beef jerky are left inside.

I start to put my things back in my backpack and see something that startles me.

I pull out a feather.

Chapter 24

I t's Saturday morning. I've been waiting for this day.

Mom is driving Alana and me down to the Pike Place Market. It is a super-fun place to walk around for hours and see fresh-from-the-ocean seafood, pastries, fruits, flowers, and crafts, plus do great people watching. After we spend some time at the market, we will catch a ferryboat over to Bainbridge Island and hang out there.

Mom drops us off, and we go get breakfast at a Seattle waterfront restaurant with a view of the sound. We both order French toast. I tell Alana about my time travel back to a time when I was a Black cowboy, and I described all the cowboys I saw who resembled people I know.

"Oh, so you didn't see anyone who looked like me? No girl or woman? It sounds like your time travel was a bit male-dominated. What, your last time travel had no use for females?" Alana makes sure I see her exaggerated side-eye look as she sits across from me.

We laugh. I feel her lightly step on my shoes.

"Really, Alana. You stepped on my clean, three-tone bowling shoes."

"Your shoes are not as adorable as I am. But, seriously, Marley, and I mean this, I don't know if you can or do want to stop taking time travels, but I'm frightened for you. Something could happen to your life.

"Something weird happened to me, when I was sitting with my mom as we were going over the classes I signed up for the first semester of ninth grade. I felt a shaking inside me, like I could fall over, but my mom never noticed. She felt nothing. She almost wanted to take me to the doctor. I wonder about that time travel to where we barely escaped trouble in the desert. Is it connected to that time when we were on your deck and you asked me whether I felt a trembling? I didn't then. But after our travel, just the other day, I felt... Well, I'm not sure *what* it was..."

"Maybe. Maybe they are connected. After each time travel, I experience trembling days later, too. I had one in the car on the way down here, and I could see you and my mom seemed normal, as if nothing was happening."

"Marley, it is your life, and I'm the only one who knows this is happening. I've told you before that you're my best friend. My mom loves you, too, and knows you watch out for me. Your mom and dad love you, and your sisters adore you as their big brother, because you protect them. You are so patient with them, when you teach them things. What am I going to do, if something happens to you? Like, what if you don't return?"

I reply, "Everything you've said tells me that I need to stop. I started with a desire to know about history, and that made me push some boundaries. But yes, I need to stop. The history taught in school has mostly been about dates, places, leaders, presidents, rulers, dictators, and wars. I want to know about ordinary people who lived during earlier times. I wonder how did everyday life disturb, distress, or motivate them to make a change? How come some of them decided to act and no longer put up with injustice?

"I'm curious about people like the Black man, Eli Whitney, who invented the cotton gin. The cotton gin removed seeds from cotton, but the invention negatively affected the enslaved. More slave labor was needed to grow and pick the cotton. Then slave life became more violent to their bodies and souls, when they suffered from harsher treatment.

"Time travel helped me understand the common person's life during those times I visited. But you are right, it is too dangerous. And what about if I found a girlfriend way back when?"

She wants to laugh a little, I think. "Oh, you've got jokes in the middle of something serious." She pushes her shoe on top of mine slightly harder. "And if you go back in time and find a girlfriend, she might be swinging from a tree and scratching an itchy behind."

"Why do you have to go there?" I try to roll my eyes at Alana, but she looks out the window while laughing.

"You started it."

"Okay, okay. I can read more without thinking I need to time travel. I can research more and inquire about more information from authorities with knowledge. I was frightened, too. But how do I stop it from happening? I don't need any more time travel. I need to talk to that old lady librarian. I know she knows what's happening. I don't wanna time travel, and I have to tell her I want to stop."

"Marley, you'll be doing the right thing to stop taking time travels." There are glints of fear in Alana's eyes.

We sit quietly and look over the water while we finish our breakfast. We watch ferryboats crossing back and forth over Puget Sound. When Alana stands up, I can tell she's still upset. I hope to change how she feels in a little while.

We walk down to the Native American booth, where the older Native American woman has made necklaces for me to give to Alana and my mother. I have the last of the money I owed, and I come to pay.

The woman is not at the booth, though. But a younger woman is there, and I tell her about the necklaces I had made.

"Yes, I am aware. You are Marley, right?"

"Yes, I am."

"My friends call me Freshlee." Her voice is full of joy. "I have two necklaces here made for you by mother. She told me about them. Here."

I take into my hand the handmade jewelry. It makes me feel rich, because they look expensive as well as so pretty. "This is most beautiful turquoise. And these orange stones—your mother told me it is called carnelian. Set with black onyx and silver and small pieces of bronze." They have all come together as a stunning gift.

Alana cups her hands over her mouth and makes little squeaks.

The young woman reaches out, touches Alana's hand, and smiles at me. "My mother wants you to feel that good things happen to good people. She told me to return all the money you already paid. You owe nothing for these items. All you owe her is to tell the truth to womenfolk. That is what she requested for payment."

"Is she here?" I ask. "I'd love for her to meet Alana. If not, can I write her a thank-you note?"

The young woman bows her head. "My mother is no longer here. She has flown higher than eagles to join our ancestors. But what she has left me is invaluable. She brought me into this world on this date thirty years ago, and on this day, I gift you in return."

Alana's tears trickle down her cheeks. My heart races at all the many revelations in my life. I must do as the Native American woman expects of me.

I place the necklace around Alana to wear. I have the other, which is a different design but very pretty. It will be for my mother to wear.

Chapter 25

Alana and I walk around Pike Place Market. We love to see all the fresh fruit, which tastes so sweet as the vendors let us taste samples. Our moods are much better, after seeing lots of crafts from leather and jewelry and all types of art.

Later, we watch the tossing of giant salmon flying about like footballs. We laugh, watch tourists, mystified at the skills of the marketplace's fish vendors.

Then, as we walk down to the ferry dock, Alana stops me at the crosswalk.

"Marley, we should think of a way to encourage others to think about history because of how important it is."

"I know, right? Let's think of what we can do. I do not want to time travel anymore, and I don't want to feel these tremors. I have had enough. I want to stay in the here and now. So, by the end of the day, let's come up with an idea."

"Green light."

"Red light."

"No, silly, I mean the thought that we need to come up with a plan is a green light."

"It's a green light now, too! And you think you're so slick."

We walk to the ferry dock to catch a ferry over to Bainbridge Island. Once we get there, we can walk around the parks. Also, there's a small movie theater on the island. And then, hopefully, we'll be in time to catch a ferry back to Seattle near sunset.

After we watch a movie and walk back to the ferry, sure enough, we catch it just as the sun is setting. The water is blue with streaks of red. I can see Alki Beach, where my dad had me run in the sand. I can hardly see the beach from our boat, it's so far away, but I can see the tall apartment buildings that look out over the beachfront.

After leaving the booth of the Native American woman and talking about history, Alana and I keep our conversation light, funny, and playful. We both wanted to have a fun day, and it has been.

We stand out on the bow of the ferryboat, feeling the warm breeze.

"Marley," Alana says, "have you thought about how we can help people like our classmates and people our age understand why history is important?"

"I think we can help others think about history if we write historical fiction. We are both good writers. We love to write. So, let's create a story people will love to read. We will need to do a lot of research, too. I like that role."

"I like that idea. Us writing a story of our historical perspective of what we know and imagine—that could be a great story. Let's add some fantasy to the story, too."

"Yeah, let's add some illusionary images."

"You know, the library has a young writer contest where they give prizes. They will also put the winners of each category in print."

"The summer is almost over," I say, "so let's get started, because I'm sure we will have plenty of homework when school starts."

Once we are back on the Seattle side, I call my mom. She and Dad pick us up. This has been one of the best days I've had in a long time.

Although I've been on restriction, my parents have seen my attitude change, and so they've allowed me some freedoms. My summer has left me with some complicated situations at times, but I've learned about my family, friendships, and why I need to take all my education seriously, as a future need.

I've also learned to take responsibility and lead when it's time.

Chapter 26

We start writing our story every afternoon, sitting out on the back deck. We Google websites for information and double-check multiple resources that lead to us having discussions of our ideas. We fall into a nice writing groove, using Alana's tablet and my laptop.

We check out books from the library, and on each trip to the library, I look for the old librarian, but I don't see her. I don't think much of it, though. There have been quite a few times when I didn't see her when I went to the library over the summer.

This afternoon, I go to the library to return some books and check out a few more. I take a seat and think, let me sit here for a while and see if I see the older woman librarian. I finally walk up to the front desk to ask the younger librarian about her and find out what days she might be in at work.

There, it dawns on me: I never knew her name. My parents taught me always introduce myself, but I don't remember introducing myself to the old librarian. I never said, "Ms. Somebody…" All I had ever said was, "Hello, ma'am." But I never called her a name.

"Hello. I was wondering, have you seen the older librarian who pushes the cart around?"

"Who?" The younger lady looks at me strangely. "What are you asking?"

"You know, the older librarian, the short lady who tends to wear white ruffled blouses. She has white almost silver hair."

"What is your name?" she asks me.

"Marley Tingle."

"Marley, you've been coming in here for a long time. I've seen you maybe a couple of times a week. I don't know what to say to you, because I don't know any older librarian or anyone like the person you have described."

Now *I* don't know what to say to her, other than to keep it moving. "Excuse me," I reply. "I'm sorry to bother you."

Then I walk away, embarrassed but more confused than anything. I know who I have seen and talked to since the start of summer. Alana met and spoke to the older woman librarian, too. And she gave me books to read, taught me history, and shared very specific, important wisdom.

I see another librarian pushing a cart, and I make my way over to her. I look over my shoulder to ensure the other librarian isn't watching me from the desk. I do not want to be thought of as harassing the library staff. I need to be able to keep coming here.

I ask her the same question about the older woman librarian and receive the same response.

"No, we don't have a librarian like the person you described."

I make my way back over to the chair where I usually sit. There is a comic book on the table. I chuckle at the fact that that was how I met the older librarian. She used to tell me I needed to read books instead of comics.

I pick the comic up, as it is my favorite comic book, one about Black Panther. I turn the pages but I'm not really reading them, because I feel lost in thought about what has happened.

I flip to the middle of the comic book, and there is a folded piece of paper with my name is on it: Mr. Marley Tingle. I open the folded paper.

Marley, I have found you to be a good student. You have made great strides in becoming someone to admire. You have applied yourself, and I know you will not allow anything or anyone to imprison your mind or any part of your being.

I ask of you, please, don't ask anything more about me. Remember, I asked you only to ask me about books. There is no need to add confusion to things where you are already confused. No one here is going to know who I am or that I even existed. I was real to you, not a dream or fantasy. You have been where you have been. You did time travel, you were a part of early history, and you did the right thing each time.

You will no longer feel those tremors you and your friend Alana have experienced. The tremors were because, each time you traveled back in time, when you returned, you were a few milliseconds off. During the tremors, time was being corrected. No worries. You are back on time. Yes.

Goodbye, young man.

Your travels are your passage to your future.

I fold the letter. My eyes are wet. What has happened to me?

I take a slow walk home. Alana comes by to work on our story. I don't have the books I was going to check out. I tell her what happened when I asked about the old woman librarian. Then, I hand her the letter.

"Why are you handing me a blank piece of paper?"

I look, and my name is not there. There is nothing inside the paper, either. I explain to her what transpired.

"Marley, you're free, and I'm free," she says after thinking about it. "We're safe now, and that's all that really matters. Let's apply ourselves to writing our story."

"I guess you are right."

"Marley, I just thought of something. The Holocaust was between 1940 and 1945. We have to think about it how long ago that was, and how old was your old librarian when she received her tattoo from the Nazis? How long ago was it for her? How old would she be now?"

"Could she still be a librarian pushing a book cart around the library?"

Chapter 27

Alana and I finish writing our story just as our summer vacation ends. We are pretty proud of our work. We let our parents and my grandparents read our work of art, and they love what we did.

When school starts, we kind of set it aside for a while, doing everything else we need to do. We want to get an impressive start on our ninth-grade year. I volunteer at the study hall to help others with their schoolwork, especially the basketball players. I encourage them, so they will be eligible to start this season, when it comes around. I also head to the gym each day before school and after study hall, to play hoops and hit the weight room.

The training my dad put me through this summer and the work I did on my own, lifting weights, is paying off. I am filling out. I was a little thin before, but now my muscle definition shows and my jump is higher. and I know I'm quicker and stronger.

Alana is elected our class president, and I help her in any way possible. When basketball season starts, I make varsity and am the starting point guard. Playing the point is new for me, but I've always been a good passer, and because of my dribbling skills, I rarely make a mistake of giving it to the other team.

Coach Barker works hard with me, and we are undefeated halfway through the season. I am averaging a nice double-digit figure. Frenchie leads the league in scoring, and college scouts are at every game to see him. A few scouts speak to my parents, praise my skill set, and say I play older than my years.

Jamelle averages a few more points than I do. I love setting him up for his sweet jumper. We get along fine now, and all the other players fall in place as a team.

We have a team come to our gym that is ranked fifth in the state. They are also undefeated, but we win the game at the end. They cannot stop Frenchie. And I hit two free throws to seal the game.

After the game, Alana comes up to me, and she's super-happy. I think she's cheerful because our team won and I played well. But then she hands me a paper about an award. It has both our names printed on it. We have won the citywide library award for best historical fiction! And we have won more than just our age group. We won for overall best writers. There is going be an award ceremony. I hug her.

"Marley, look what we did!"

The next day, we share the news with our principal and our counselors, and they put it in the school newspaper. We plan to share this with our spirit assembly next week, too.

The following week, the day after we beat our crosstown rivals, Alana and I go to the award ceremony. The person who heads the citywide library system presents us with the award, and we shake hands with the mayor.

A woman and a man approach Alana and me as we take some pictures together. They ask to meet our parents. They tell our parents and us that they are from one of the universities I hope will offer me a basketball scholarship one day. These two people represent the language arts department. They will provide us full-academic scholarships, if our grades stay up, even though we are only freshmen.

I want to play college basketball, and my game keeps evolving. One day, I'll be a senior, and I hope colleges take notice. I'm hoping for that opportunity. But now, what I already have is that Alana and I wrote something to inspire others and to teach them how history is vital to everyone's lives.

It's amazing how my being grounded for a whole summer was undesirable, but it turned into something so beneficial to my life and others.

I will always be curious and mystified about the time travels in my life. However, all the lessons I learned blotted out the negatives and turned my journey into a positive.

A NEW LAND

A Historical Fiction with Fantasy

Written by Marely Barton Tingle and Alana Kona Parks

The prettiest woman ever created walked the Earth long before any explorers journeyed out from the lands of Africa or Europe. Her name was Hubun, Queen of the River. Her skin was a flaming, smoldering black and seemed hotter than the Sahara Desert. Often revered as the most advanced woman in the universe, no one would challenge the claim.

Huban led lion-drawn carriages and carts along the Niger River from one end to the other. She traveled in a covered chariot that housed her bed and stored goods. Her covered chariot also carried ways to cook and store foods. She made weapons and tools and anything else needed to survive.

She could capture her food or kill her enemy without fear. Enemies feared her for what she could do, but no one feared her, because she had not one single bone of evil in her body.

Huban was a healer, not a wounder. She was not a war starter but a war ender. And she was an alliance creator, not a separator.

Her most treasured skill advanced the world: working a potter's wheel and molding clay. She made the most coveted pots, urns, and basins of every size. Her works were in high demand in every village along the river. The queen could take clay and mold vessels to travel the Nile and maybe far into the uncharted oceans.

Yearly, she made her way along the tributaries to furnish other kings and queens. She ensured that even the feeblest and humblest of villagers received her best. The Queen of the River Nile shared her knowledge and hired, from each village, young women to help spread her great works. She taught them to gain wealth through facts and wisdom, so they could earn gold, silver, bronze, commodities, and land through the skills she taught them. Most of all, she decreed giving and love in the light of the meaning of her name, Huban.

Through her travels along the Nile River of 4,100 miles and the Niger river of 2,600 miles, the queen edified how to use the fertile regions for abundance. She sowed and harvested yams, Oryza rice, and pearl millet to make bhakri flatbread. She prepared the people to live and thrive under the sun and moon, from planting and fishing.

With her teaching and shared experience, she helped create trade centers along the great rivers. In the Niger bend region, she brought people together in peace to encourage trans-Saharan trade. This venture designed and created wealth for the Ghana, Mali, and Timbuktu empires.

From the Mediterranean Sea and down through the Blue Nile and White Nile, she enjoined fellowship with the cities of Cairo, Aswan, Giza, Khartoum, Jinja, and the countries of Egypt and Sudan. All rivers became centers of education and philosophy, art, music, and literature and produced refinement in cultivation. As the Queen of all Rivers, she brought together Muslims and Christians to respect and embrace residing as one people for the betterment of all.

The Queen of the River—no one knew her age, as she embodied generations and had lived ageless in her work and image—placed her lifelong work in every tributary of the river. Huban often rested near the river's delta on the Gulf of Guinea, where the Great Ocean swallowed the flow of the Niger River. She slept at the delta's end, listening to the songs of the great ocean wash ashore. Her eyes traced the stars with a fire, sending burning embers and casting light high in the sky, while her heart longed for a king.

A village of maidens surrounded her in the warm evening sunset. The young women sang songs Huban had taught them. They hummed low, but in both unison and harmony.

Then, she told the story of the man who was set afloat in a vessel he and she had crafted, in hopes of finding a new world. He was to come back one day, but he had not made his way after days, months, and years. She believed he was gone forever. Her tale had moments where the young women dreamed with delight, wishing for a warrior to come to protect them.

The young women listen to Huban. Was it a fable, a myth, or imaginary truth? They did not care; they loved listening to the queen...

He was from Senegal on the banks of the Gambia River. A great man named Maad. He was a master of land and rivers. He could swim against the current of raging tempestuous floods. He could climb the highest peaks and subdue creatures that could rip the skin or poison any other man. River monsters swam away from him, knowing he could strangle them and end their existence.

He was a leader who made the Greeks and the Romans seek peace from of whomever came to conquer. Maad defeated them with only a few warriors each time, as he had developed methodologies unknown to brutish-thinking men. The kings in every region gathered and asked him to map the world.

He traveled along the coast of our people, who transformed from shades of light to dark from north to south, and he crossed over the lands many times from east to west. He chronicled each species living and the maturation of its existence. He made alliances for trade as he made trails over hills and mountains and through the jungles.

Maad found me as a young woman who had lived in the wilderness. I was under the Victoria Falls in Zimbabwe when he walked in the wash and asked us to make an alliance to make the world a better place. Instantly, we began to share knowledge of the skies and the deep waters.

Our united strength was like stone mountains, and we moved as fast as leopards in need of food. We commanded the water river and land to swirl around us as a fortification wherever we walked.

We traveled to all points of the lands where the people of all skins resided and even blue-eyed people. We broke bread among the coal-colored magnificent beauties and had stories to share. He camped on top of Kilimanjaro in Tanzania and under the Red Sea to build dreams. We swam across Lake Victoria as if we were majestic sea creatures and spread our arms to glide amongst the clouds lifting the sun.

A message came from kings and queens from many regions. They asked Maad to find new lands—a new world across the Great Ocean that the sun showed far away. North of the Mediterranean, where people with the fairest skin lived, there was an assumption that the world is flat. If so, one would fall off the end into a pit of darkness and never be found or saved. Yet we had always known the moon circles around our world. Our people believe in the sun and the moon, and we all turn in cycles that bring dawn and dusk. As a people, we learned medicine and sciences and reasons for being, and we didn't live in fear.

Maad asked me to use my potter's wheel to craft an unsinkable sailing vessel. He dug deep into the ground and made a kiln to fire the clay. I agreed to help. I only wanted for him no less than I wanted for myself.

I want to say I gave my people more than they had before. The building of the vessel and the launching were here in this delta. Maad and I dressed in white silk and walked into the Great Ocean as the sun skimmed over the water and turned red before it turned dark. We floated with our eyes scanning the stars, as I often do now.

He told me, "I must sail to a new world to bring our people ways to expand. I will find a new world and come back and take you with me to the new world. I will never forsake our friendship."

We perfected a long-distance vessel. We stored dried fruits, salted fish, and rainwater urns for months of travel. He set sail under the moonlight when the water was calm. There were two trained albatrosses onboard. Maad would release them with notes, and they would fly back here, to our home, to send a signal that he had reached another world. The birds can fly for months and land on the water to rest. We knew the birds would be the perfect transmission of the messages of his journey to the new world.

Each week, I released a thousand butterflies in his honor while waiting to hear of his safe passage. The birds returned thirty days later with no notes. Maad must have perished, lost at sea.

I am not sad as he did what the world needed him to do, which was to try. I miss his friendship, though, and I sleep talk to this woman's best friend. One day, when my eternal tranquility comes, I will join the ancestors' resting place, and then I will see him again...

The young women watched the most extraordinary woman they had ever known shed very human tears. They cried and surrounded Huban with embraces of love. They all slept next to her, pressing tightly to her, to comfort her in her sleep.

When the eastern sun came over the mountains and started to light the Great Ocean from black to blue, a mass of a million butterflies landed all over the delta. They floated in and out of the ocean tributaries. The water and land appeared all colors ever known to man, full of butterfly wings of beauty.

The maidens awoke to make coffee, sweet bread, and other nourishment for the woman they adored. They wanted her to feel love. They called Huban's name after they had prepared a feast of food. But she did not join them.

They stared at each other, not knowing what to do. Should they let her sleep? Should they wake her?

They chose the youngest of the young women to wake her, in hopes of bringing vitality. The young woman entered the dwelling and did not come back. Another young woman entered, and she did not come back. One after another, each woman joined in, and soon, they were all carrying the body of Huban held high.

The young women walked in silence, honoring the soul of the Queen of all the Rivers gone to rest. The butterflies covered the beach, as if they were waiting for a mission to lead them to their next flight.

The news traveled, and many women gathered with young and male warriors. They collectively used their learned skill of the potter's wheel and clay and kiln fire to craft a vessel to lay to rest the body of Huban at sea.

The day came, and they set her body to sail. They understood no one would bail out the hull, if high winds and rain came, and it would sink the vessel. They also believed Maad most likely had been overcome by the same fate. All accepted that the two great friends would meet at the bottom of the Great Ocean, be together, and never part again.

Many from the east, south, and north joined the western tribes and villages. They watched the Queen of all the Rivers drift out to sea. Albatrosses floated next to or flew above the vessel. The butterflies left high in the sky and wandered with the wind.

For forty days and forty nights, the ocean stayed calm, with moderate winds to float the body of Huban. The vessel sailed to a new world. Only one man had walked the shores before Huban's lifeless body was helped ashore by that one man.

Maad stood over Huban. He lifted her in his arms. When he lifted her, the sun sent vapors to her heart, and she had life again. Huban's eyes opened. Her lips parted as she stood and exhaled vapors, and they rose back to the sun.

Maad had attempted to sail back, but a great whale had breached the water, landing on his vessel, and breaking his lifeline into pieces. He had only sailed for a few days. His choice was to attempt to swim the Great Ocean for weeks in hopes of returning to his people or to swim a few days back to the new world he had found. The new world was his only choice.

The whale felt sorry for the playful act that destroyed the vessel. The whale could not stay atop the water with the hot sun, so he let Maad rest on his snout and pushed Maad while underwater. He only came above the water when both of them needed air. The whale returned Maad to the new world.

When Huban and Maad beheld each other, they appeared as the young people they once were. They took their newfound youth and began to chart a great river, which they named the Amazon. Their intellect made them understand the science on a new continent and the fact that the world is round.

They saw the sun rise over the water and the sun set over the land. They came from where the sun rose over the land and set off across the Great Ocean. They recognized many animals, but many were new or similar to those where they had once lived. Some animals were never to be tamed but were a part of the cycle of hunter and prey.

In the years to come, they ventured back to the motherland and helped many others sail over in vessels to the new world. Maad and Huban discovered the new world and helped create a new civilization.

THE END

About the Author

Alvin L.A. Horn is a national award-winning author, published by Simon and Schuster Publishing and self-publisher of six novels. An acclaimed spoken word artist/poet/musician, Alvin was born in the Pacific Northwest and credits his writing to his mother, who made him go to the library. Also, to the "little gray-haired Jewish lady, the librarian," a concentration camp survivor, for introducing him to writers such as Richard Wright and Zora Neale Hurston. Upon reading Nikki Giovanni's work, Alvin knew he wanted to be a writer of love stories, social commentary, and poetry.

Alvin works in the field of education, teaching life skills and creative writing while working with at-risk kids. His writings, ranging from fiction to nonfiction, have appeared in many periodicals for over thirty years.

In addition to the books listed below, Alvin is also a contributing author in the anthologies, *The Soul of a Man 2* and *The Soul of a Man, 3*, as well as a writer for the *Inner-City News* and a feature writer for Real Life *Real Faith Magazine*. He has written essays for several national newspapers and magazines, including the Seattle local paper, *The Seattle Emerald. The Flava News*, awarded the Unsung Peoples Poet Laureate to Alvin L.A. Horn.

Find him Alvin L.A. Horn at www.alvinhorn.com

2001: *Poems from My Dresser Drawer*, the poem "Trembling"; winner of a National Poetry Award and Best Poem, by The Flava Poetry Coffee House Association

2006: *Brush Strokes*. Romantic Blues Publishing. A fictional story of one's past painting the present and future through a romantic journey.

2006 AALA award for Best Romance Novel

Ebony Magazine Top Ten Novel of the Year

Heart & Soul Magazine Best New Writer

2012: *Perfect Circle*, published by Simon and Schuster Publishing, and Zane Imprint. Released as a Simon and Schuster Publishing Hottest New Writer; reached national bestseller status. About stalking, violence, and philandering in the Emerald City.

2014*: One Safe Place*, published by Simon and Schuster Publishing and Zane Imprint. About how friends and foes, politicians and romantic interests intersect with crime in the Emerald City. The novel reached national bestseller status.

2015 – The Soul of a Man 2: Make Me Wanna' Holler, (Peace in the Storm Publishing) an anthology of essays concerning the Black man in America – featured essay

2016: Rerelease of *Brush Strokes*, Romantic Blues Publishing, with an added short story. A fictional story of one's past painting the present and future through a journey back from where it all started.

2017: *Bad Before Good & Those In Between*, Romantic Blues Publishing. About mystery and suspense in Seattle along the streets of hidden truths of the past and present.

2019: *Heart & Home*, Romantic Blues Publishing. A historical mystery and suspense fiction about a Negro soldier from Seattle coming home from World War II.

2021: *Journey to Love*, Romantic Blues Publishing. The crossing of lives of the past and present of a ninety-year-old Serene May and her caretaker, Blunie Rivers aka Blu. Serene encourages Blu to read her journal of her life and times and teaches him how to search and to hold onto love.

All in available in paperback and E-book

Acknowledgments

My Creator, thank you for giving me the opportunity to write and to be read by many. I hope I made you laugh at some of the ill-advised things I have done. Through your grace, my gifts have been given a chance for all to see.

I give thanks to Big Mama, my grandmother, and to all the elders, women who have taught me the value of the love of a woman, each in their own way. I'm blessed to have had all of you touch me in your individual ways. I write about women like you—the textured fabric of life I have been wrapped in.

To the men who helped shape me in the mode of who I am, without ever knowing the impact you have had on me. Whether you were my bloodline or a mentor, I have watched you for how to be my best, as a man. I love the old soul I am, creating the Renaissance man I am, so I pen layers of storylines.

I walk humbly, knowing my writings bring awareness to the struggles that this world places as burdens on everyone, as we try to make better the world for our children. Every woman and man handles the weight of mankind differently, creating the narratives I write and will write.

To the friends and family very dear to me, as the song says, "We go a long way back." Even if it's not true, thank you. Each one of you somewhere along the way has loved me in your special way, helping me to stay on course or to get back to where I needed to be, I thank you for that.

To my son, Ivan, and daughter, Danielle, my nephews and nieces and grandchildren, somewhere along the way each one of you has loved me in your special way, helping me to be grounded and true to myself. I thank you.

To my editor on this project, Kathryn F. Galan at Wynnpix Productions, thanks. You are a real pro. Besides editing, you teach along the way.

My Seattle family of friends, *Please to Be* is you, as we are often multiethnic in our bloodlines, and diverse in our friendships. We are rain and the bluest skies, the fresh ocean air, and snow-topped mountains that can and do blow up. We are rivers and streams in the middle of our neighborhoods, and fresh fish and crab, and shrimp.

We are Rainier Beach, Duwamish-Tukwila, Beacon Hill, Rainier Valley, and, in the CD, Renton, Skyway, Mountlake, Capitol Hill, Mount Baker, Leschi, Madrona, West Seattle, South Park, White Center, Kent, Burien, and farther south. We are strolling around Seward Park, Alki, Coulon Beach, Green Lake.

We are Jimi Hendrix, Bruce Lee, Quincy Jones, Bill Russell, Marshawn Lynch-Beast Mode, and rain and sun, mountains and oceans. We are Vikings, Quakers, Bulldogs, and Eagles. We are the Seattle Super Sonics forever!

To the students and athletes, I taught and coached over the years, I can't thank you enough for teaching me. I send a shout out to all the students I have encountered at South Shore K-8, and to all the Seattle south-end students.

My style

As regards my style, I have very limited ability to hand-write with a pen or pencil. Plain and simple, I cannot take a pencil and write more than a few sentences without writing them backward or writing letters backward, yet it looks correct to me.

Why? I have a learning disorder; my brain waves get confused, and it comes out through my writing hand. Yet I could read and comprehend at a high level in school. Teachers and school counselors would marvel at my verbal test scores, when allowed.

The name for my disability is *dysgraphia*. Dysgraphia involves me having difficulty with my fine motor skills and motor memory. I know what I want to write, but by the time the signal reaches my fingers holding a pencil, it's a mess.

In the Sixties and Seventies, before special education, if you were a nice kid, they just passed you along in many cases. Who cares if he can't seem to spell? He can sing, dance, play instruments, and recite poetry. I played the lead roles in all our plays, and by the time I was in high school, I was on the sports field, playing sports at a high level, so I was passed along. Now, of all the people in the world, for years I have worked in education. Go figure.

How? Well, finally, as I really wanted to write the poems, short stories, and novels like you will read here, I got over my embarrassment and sought help. First, I was able to get a correct diagnosis when I was in my late thirties. Then, I learned a system of calm and how to limit stress, sometimes through white noise or music playing. As long as I use a keyboard, I do all right. I'm like many people whose mind types faster than their fingers; with me, often my mind will type pages before my fingers catch up. I've learned to laugh at myself from my heart, instead of letting my mind beat up on me for what I can't do. And I celebrate what I can do.

My disabilities, in many ways, have created my style of writing, much like the way a blind person sees life another way and certain of their senses reroute, thus creating a style. It's like listening to Stevie Wonder play drums. He hits the drums on the right beat, but he hits different drums on those beats, which is much different from other drummers. His drumming sounds unique but still correct. I hope you keep enjoying my gift, and my style.

For our children's sake

Often, our children may seem to be slow learners or have issues in school. It's easy to blame the system or the teachers. Well, look at them, too, but also look a little deeper and wider.

A parent's pride or embarrassment should never stand in the way of helping a child achieve. The blame game does nothing down the road. Like most children, I learned to mask or distract from most of my learning disability.

I recited most of my English/language arts schoolwork to classmates, and they wrote my work down for me; in return, they got to copy from my imagination or mental retention for their own assignments. My conversational skills on multiple subjects with adults often blinded them to my other shortcomings. Often, children with high IQs mask the most problems.

If your child is disengaged in the learning, the class clown, picks on other kids for their shortcomings, has to be forced to read, and many other telltale signs that something is not right, look deeper and be vigilant. Don't ever say I've done all I could.

Maybe your child needs glasses or has hearing problems or even has bad teeth that may keep that child from wanting to talk in front of the class. These may seem minor things to you, but may be major to your child. There can be any number of reasons to slow a child's progress. Kids tend to act out in many different ways to mask their problems. Most of all, they don't know how to tell us what is going on inside of them.

Let us all work together.

Books mentioned in Places to Be

The Royal Kingdoms of Ghana, Mali, and Songhay: Life in Medieval Africa, by Patricia McKissack and Fredrick McKissack.

Zenzele: A Letter for My Daughter. By J. Nozipo Maraire"

Black Indians: A Hidden Heritage, by William Katz."

Black Cowboys of the Old West by Tricia Martineau Wagner.

Animal Farm, by By George Orwell.

The Ways of White Folks, by Langton Hughes

The Diary of Anne Frank, by Anne Frank

King Peggy, by Peggielene Bartels

Made in the USA
Monee, IL
07 June 2022

c6eea0e8-d187-42be-96a2-6f5a32d301b9R01